THE BERMUDA BOND

By the same author:

Fiction
All Through the Night
Keeping the Lid On
Spy Without a Cause
and
The Missing Monsieur Max

Non-fiction
Playing Popular Piano and Keyboards

The Bermuda Bond

Neil Thomas

THOROGOOD

Published by Thorogood
10-12 Rivington Street
London EC2A 3DU

Telephone: 020 7749 4748
Email: info@thorogoodpublishing.co.uk
Web: www.thorogoodpublishing.co.uk

This is a work of fiction. Names, characters, businesses,
places, events, locales, and incidents are either the products
of the author's imagination or used in a fictitious manner.
Any resemblance to actual persons, living or dead, or actual
events is purely coincidental.

A CIP catalogue record for this book is available
from the British Library.

ISBN paperback: 978 185418 9363
ISBN eBook: 978 185418 9370

Designed by: Driftdesign Ltd
www.getyourdrift.com

For Cheryl and our own Bermuda bond, 14.10.93

Who's Who

Owen Ash, known as Ash	MD, Ashbury Events Ltd, London
Gavin Boatwright	Owner of Oxford Beaches, Bermuda
Doug Bonsall	Journalist on *The Royal Bugle*, Bermuda
Selwyn Brookes	Senior Partner, Copthorne & Brookes, Bermuda
Wallace Copthorne	Partner, Copthorne & Brookes; Director of Copthorne & Brookes Reinsurance (CaBRe), Bermuda
Beatrice 'Bee' Goode	IT Consultant, Bermuda

Dawn Grainger	Events Director, Ashbury Events Ltd, London
Harriet Hall	Ex-employee of Ashbury Events Ltd, London
Linda LaFong	Ex-wife of Gavin Boatwright, Bermuda
Dorian Miller	Guest Curator and Historian-in-Residence at the Royal Naval Dockyard, Bermuda
Carey Merino	Investigator, FBI, New York
Tony Merino	Brother of Carey Merino and Director, Lehman Brothers, New York
Fiona Peters	Wife of Mike Peters
Mike Peters	Partner, Copthorne & Brookes; Director of CaBRe, Bermuda
Anthony de Rivaulx QC	Tax and Commercial Barrister, Gray's Inn, London

Scott Roberts	Inspector, Bermuda Police Service
Ben Sanchez	Technical Consultant, Ashbury Events Ltd, London
Raymond White	Senior Partner, Lemon, Lockhart & White, Bermuda
Edward 'Fast Eddie' Wilkins	Lawyer, sole practitioner with Wilkins Legal and Associate of Cogence Inc, London

The setting is the 1990s

Prologue

Torrential rain was beating against the roof of his black cab, its windows so misted up you couldn't tell where on earth you were. The windscreen wipers were noisily losing their battle with nature. They were doing little more than providing a backing rhythm to *I'll Remember April*, being played on Jazz FM radio, surprisingly, by the cabbie who was, unsurprisingly, talking loudly over it.

'This is the great Erroll Garner. Did you know that he was so short that, when he performed, he sat on a copy of the Manhattan phone directory that he carried around with him?'

It was like being driven around London by the gratingly erudite jazz pundit, Benny Green. And that would have been more enjoyable than what followed.

*　　　*　　　*

11

Owen Ash – Ash to his friends – was sitting at a table near the fugged-up windows of Rules restaurant in Maiden Lane. Opposite Ash sat a ruddy-faced, multi-jowled, shiny-headed accountant of great seniority – fact, and importance – his opinion. This large man was mid-sixtyish, but easily passing as older, and he appeared uncomfortably out of place in the way that a pompous expat does when on leave in the old country. Back in the UK from Bermuda, this partner in Copthorne & Brookes – a leading island firm of insurance and reinsurance auditors – rejoiced under the name of Wallace Copthorne and looked exactly how you'd expect a Bermudian accountant to look. Ash would describe him by saying his doppelganger was Colonel Hall, the one with the hangdog face on the Phil Silvers show. From a respected family on the island, Wallace Copthorne was a big fish there and this meeting was beneath him by a long way. He hated being deep down with the bottom feeders.

The conversation was stilted until Copthorne had consumed the best part of a second bottle of house claret. After boasting about his latest exciting exploits in corporate liquidations, yes really, he got round to discussing the main reason for the lunch – the big conference that Ash's company, Ashbury Events, organised with Copthorne & Brookes every two years. As soon as he raised the subject, Copthorne turned nasty, his cheeks reddened and his patience seemingly ran out. From the sideways look of pure hatred he was given across the table, it was obvious to Ash that he had just been mentally moved from the assets to the liabilities side of Wallace Copthorne's personal balance sheet.

'I still keep asking myself why the hell we should share the profits with you?' Copthorne asked straight out, the mellowing effect of having eaten his favourite dish of steak and kidney pie being evidently short-lived. Ash knew the accountant in Copthorne had been totting up the debits throughout the lunch and had obviously failed to find any credits in the process. This was an old bleat, and Ash had been expecting to hear it again at some point over lunch.

The red plush seating, the polished wood, the gilt-framed pictures and the starched white linen gave the perfect setting for this old duffer who boasted he only ever dined at Rules when he was in town. It was his natural habitat and, until that point, he had been wallowing in it like an old hippo at his favourite watering hole.

Wallace Copthorne had an arrogance that had been bred into him by being from one of the oldest families on Bermuda, and he boasted of its continuous residency on the island as far back – he claimed – as the seventeenth century. Privilege and superiority were ingrained in him, and that's how he presented himself to allcomers. It was never mentioned that slavery and the tobacco trade of the early years had been the basis of their wealth because, fortunately, the family had also been very astute in profiting even more from the post-war development of the territory as an offshore financial centre.

Accountancy was considered a safe haven for any male Copthorne not quite bright enough to become a lawyer and Wallace had been duly despatched to Canada to qualify, it being deemed by his father easier for him to do so there than it would have been in London. As a boy before that, naturally, he had been harshly educated at some minor public school in England, just to make sure any soft edges were sharpened up and to give him that air of effortless superiority.

How should the question Copthorne raised be replied to? Ash knew it was impertinent and intended to be, but even so, to answer it as bluntly as it had been put would be sure to bring the relationship between their firms to a premature end.

Of course, touchiness goes hand in hand with bullying and Ash knew that Copthorne was always quick to take offence. You can't call it sensitivity in a domineering man like him, it was more of an instant outrage at being questioned, challenged, disagreed with, or contradicted. Tempted though he was to respond with what he really thought of him and to tell him to get stuffed, Ash went into professional diplomatic mode as, unfortunately, there was a lot riding on the next joint event taking place with the continued involvement of Copthorne & Brookes.

'We've built up a good relationship over the years – a good marriage of experience and expertise – and we're going from strength to strength.'

'We've put too much time into this. It's cost us far more than we've ever got out of it,' Copthorne said.

'That's been the case for us too, but all that changed with the last event. It would be mad to kill it off just when it's starting to generate a hefty return as well as new business for you and your partners.'

'We want an 80/20 split of profits in our favour and we want Harriet Hall re-employed to run it. You need a pretty girl to keep the delegates on side. Those are my conditions.'

It had been inevitable that Copthorne would raise both issues. He'd always banged on about wanting a bigger slice of the cake and Ash knew that *they* were hopping mad that Harriet was no longer working on what they always claimed was *their* biennial Bermuda bash. Ash decided it was pointless to beat about the bush. He needed to be direct and pull no punches.

'Neither of your conditions is going to be possible to meet. We can always do the conference with one of your rivals on the island if you'd prefer. They've all been in touch with us umpteen times touting for the chance to take it off your hands.'

'You're not going to budge? We can do it ourselves, you know. We can do it for this year's event. We've got the time and the contacts. We're better placed than you are to run the whole show. We can easily find some conference wallahs to run it. Maybe even get Harriet back to work on it for us.'

'No, we're not going to give it all up to you, I'm afraid. You've forgotten a few basics, like the marketing and the venue, for example. We've got all the mailing lists and the best hotel on the island for such a prestigious event as this is booked by us for years ahead, so we could run it with ... maybe Clifford and Gotch. Either we keep to the same terms as before and do it with you or ... we'll have to go our separate ways. Your call.'

This shot seemed to stop Copthorne in his tracks and Ash was glad he'd loaded that particular elephant gun in advance of the meeting, having had a premonition over-night that it was likely to prove something of a showdown.

Neither of them said anything for what seemed like ages, and Ash was damned if he was going to fill the silence – as he usually would – in order to plug an awkward gap in a conversation.

Who would blink first was the game they were each playing. In the end, Ash won.

'Well ... I guess we'd better make it work, then,' said Copthorne, 'but it won't be with *me* directly involved any longer. You'll have to deal with one of our other less senior partners, Mike Peters. That'll suit both of us, I'm sure. What?'

This made Ash smile, inwardly, as he knew that Peters did all the grunt work for Copthorne & Brookes on the event anyway, so no change there. Plus, he now knew a lot more about Peters and his reasons for wanting a closer involvement.

Ash had always known it was better to get to a middle-ranker if you wanted to get things done. There was a hierarchy of laziness in most professional partnerships, especially in places like Bermuda, and those at the top couldn't be bothered with detail.

'Obviously, as you're fully aware, I know Mike well, so, yes, I think that'll work.'

Thankfully, Wallace Copthorne did not call Ash's bluff. Typical bully, he was all bluster. A man of many chins, all of them weak, thought Ash as he was left to pick up the tab when Copthorne, in a foul mood, left the restaurant moaning about the rain in London when, in truth, it rains more on Bermuda.

He asked for the bill and ordered himself a coffee. What a lunch. Ash knew that Copthorne considered his manner too louche for the serious business of international accountancy and probably counted himself lucky to confine most of his business dealings with those less like Ash and more like himself.

Ash mused that, ideally, Copthorne would like to have him tarred and feathered or, better still, served up along with the jugged hare and capercaillie at a private dinner at Rules for the men in suits he normally dined with.

Meanwhile, the waiter handling the bill's payment speculated – as he usually did – on the likely relationship between the two diners. Godfather and godson perhaps? No, the lunch had seemed too acrimonious for that to be the case. Maybe father and son, then, arguing about the son joining the family firm, a battle between conformity and creativity. Dad in his seventies? Blazer, shirt and tie. Son in his thirties? Jacket, shirt and tie put on as a duty? One a die-hard, old-school capitalist pig, and the other more of a long-haired lefty trying to break free? Chalk and cheese, in other words. The father cantankerous, the son freewheeling. They're bound to go their separate ways, he thought. Christmas must be fun at their house.

As Ash looked at the pouring rain outside, drinking his coffee and contemplating the year ahead, he couldn't help wondering how – with so many fascinating characters like Charles Dickens, Graham Greene and Laurence Olivier being regulars at Rules over the years – he'd ended up lunching there with someone like Wallace Copthorne.

PART ONE

BERMUDA & LONDON
1994

1.

BERMUDA

Born in a little village just outside Cambridge in the old mill house at Queen's Mill, Dorian Miller's first serious work of history was to write a pamphlet on the home he was born and raised in. The mill had been inhabited and worked by his family for hundreds of years until it ceased its milling activities and closed in the nineteenth century.

Succeeding generations then developed what eventually became a well-established family business of book publishers, where they were extraordinarily clever at whittling down author submissions, sorting the wheat from the chaff, and then refining a chosen text until they knew they had a bestseller on their hands.

Dorian's researches found that the house had never, ever flooded – such was the acumen of our forebears as builders – until one day when some damn fool at the

National Rivers Authority had refused to open a sluice gate downstream and caused the Cam to burst its banks. Priceless first editions stored in their riverside library had been lost as a result.

He was destined to be a historian from the moment when, aged thirteen, he held in his hand that printed monograph of *A Short History of Queen's Mill*.

Later honing his historical research skills at Peterhouse, Cambridge – chosen, naturally enough, because it was Cambridge's oldest college – he eventually emerged with a PhD. His thesis on *The Strategic Importance of the Royal Navy's Dockyards and Bases 1793-1815* was later published, in hardback, by the family firm of Fine Grain Publishing Ltd, then being run by his older brother Sebastian. The photograph on the back flap of the dust cover showed Dorian to be as typical a corduroy-jacketed academic as ever there was, but one whose bright eyes and chiselled features promised greater things to come.

The miller's trade lived on in him, 'Miller by name, miller by nature,' he liked to quip, usually adding that he loved nothing more than 'grinding the stones of history to produce finely sifted facts and opinions'.

It was hardly surprising that 'Dorian the historian' – as his brother teasingly nicknamed him as a child – ended up on Bermuda as Guest Curator and Historian-in-Residence at the Royal Naval Dockyard in Sandys Parish. He'd done vacation work as a volunteer at Chatham, Portsmouth and Devonport before becoming a junior lecturer in naval history at Southampton University. He was a shoo-in for the Bermuda Dockyard job when he'd applied for it a few years previously.

Living in his pretty pink and white cottage, a one-bedroom suite with a sea view of Mangrove Bay, once a smugglers' harbour, Dorian knew he was lucky to be based at Oxford Beaches, which was actually both a luxury hotel *and* really close to the Bermuda Dockyard.

His accommodation was provided free because the wealthy owner – the aptly named, as it turned out, Gavin Boatwright – shared Dorian's obsession with nautical history and was a leading patron of the Bermuda Maritime Museum. Some evenings they would talk late into the night whilst sitting overlooking the ocean and drinking far too many a Dark 'n' Stormy, two naval nuts hitting the rum and recreating the Age of Sail.

Gavin was a handsome man in his sixties, like a silver-haired Cary Grant, who had made his fortune in the US from the leisure industries – whatever he meant by that, Dorian didn't ask – ploughing some of it into his hotel venture and enjoying frittering the rest of it away on various less successful projects.

One was a failed attempt to turn his now ex-wife, Linda LaFong, into an international novelist with her trashy bonkbuster. That cost him over one hundred and fifty thousand dollars as an investment. He foolishly paid an unscrupulous publisher to get *Love on Bermuda* into the bestseller lists, only for its author to be savaged by the critics as 'the illiterati's Jackie Collins'.

When they divorced – she cited mental cruelty, alleging he had made her a laughing stock on the island – he turned his full attention to another longer-standing pet project. This was the seemingly unending endeavour to build a replica of HMS Pickle, the famous ten-gun schooner that was purchased by the Royal Navy in 1800 from a merchant yard on Bermuda. It made its name by bringing home to England, in 1805, the news of the victory at Trafalgar.

Gavin liked Dorian because he was the first person on the island not to dismiss him as a crank and he enjoyed having a like-minded guest staying at the hotel. Gavin no longer socialised much on the island, saying he was bored to the back teeth with some of the wealthy Tucker Town expats with zero interests and nothing worthwhile to say, who sat around all day in their air-conditioned homes watching satellite TV.

*   *   *

Dorian had first met Ash in England, a few years before taking the Bermuda job, when he was booked by Ashbury Events to give a lecture on the leadership of Nelson to a group of specially invited CEOs at a fundraising dinner held in the Admiral's quarters and wardroom of HMS Victory at Portsmouth Dockyard.

They had hit it off, sharing a sense of humour, love of history and a cynical view of the supposedly top echelons of British industry. Over breakfast the following morning at Carey's Manor Hotel in the New Forest, they'd discussed the possibility of Dorian speaking at various residential senior management training events that Ash arranged there from time to time. This had proved to be a lucrative sideline for Dorian and successful for Ash's company, referenced in glowing testimonials from happy delegates.

Between them they subsequently authored a book, published, of course, by Fine Grain, with the title *Management by Naval Gazing – A Study of the Leadership Style of Admiral Lord Nelson.* With its emphasis on teamwork, defined roles, free exchange of ideas, participation in decision-making, encouragement of initiative and a shared sense of ownership, their approach had shown that Nelson could have written a modern textbook on management techniques.

Their book demonstrated that the leadership style practised by Nelson was in stark contrast to the blinkered thinking of most modern top bosses who are generally unable to face adversity with patience, see beyond the end of their noses, hold their nerve when overcoming setbacks and actually believe in what they're doing.

Needless to say, the book sank without trace because, as one well-intentioned reviewer had said, 'It's a pity that British managers don't actually read leadership books to improve their performance.'

'We should have rigged the sales better,' was Dorian's quip at the time.

Still, it had proved to be the basis of a close friendship, and although Dorian's move to Bermuda had meant that he could no longer be involved with the UK seminars, Ash was pleased that he had been able to use his friend to develop a decent partners' programme for the event they ran with Copthorne & Brookes. And it meant that Ash would have at least one loyal ally on the island.

The year before, Dorian, then newish to Bermuda, had participated in his first Bermuda conference, run by Ashbury Events in the island's capital, Hamilton.

After one of his lectures on the history of Bermuda, an attractive blonde – obviously suffering from an advanced dose of rock fever – had asked him how he got on with Ash, without even bothering to ask how well Dorian actually knew him.

'What do you make of the boss man of Ashbury Events, Mr Miller? You're one of us now, aren't you, an honorary Bermudian, an Onion, so you can speak openly with me.'

Moving up close, taking exaggerated baby steps towards him on her very high heels, she'd leaned in toward Dorian's face to hear his reply. She was, by then, close enough for him to scent the intimacy on offer and for her to watch his eyes drop to glance down at the contents of her revealing silk dress.

'I like working with him, I've –'

Before he had time to say how much he liked Ash, Mrs Fiona Peters – that's what her name badge said – had continued to put her foot in it, all the while flirting overtly. She was very forward, but the unpredictability obvious in her manner indicated an over-fondness for the bottle. She was clearly out to shock, and Dorian had realised she liked to play with people, no doubt men in general, but now him in particular.

Without any further preamble, she came out and said of Ash, 'We all hate him on the island. My husband's a partner in Copthorne & Brookes and he hasn't a good word to say for him, you know. Apparently Ash's company take all the profits and let him and his partners do all the work! Bit of a cheek, don't you think?'

Dorian then knew exactly what he was dealing with and had replied cautiously, 'Well at least they bring a lot of delegates and their partners to the island and contribute to the local economy – even giving people like me a role. That can't be all bad, can it?'

'Well, you're an academic, you wouldn't understand. Just be careful you get paid. Now, enough of all that, tell me what you like doing to unwind after one of your lectures. I'm sure I could help you relax.'

Dorian, fortunately, was able to turn away and ignore

the overt invitation because, just at that moment, he was grabbed on the arm by another 'fan' who had pushed in front of others jostling for his attention, as if the Q & A he allowed at the end of his talk wasn't enough. Flattering, or infuriating?

Dorian had reported the exchange with Fiona Peters back to Ash, who'd laughed and told him, 'Keep your ear to the ground but don't feel you have to resort to pillow talk to pick up gossip from Mrs Peters ... juicy though her titbits would undoubtedly be.'

Already knowing what Copthorne & Brookes thought of having to work with Ashbury Events, what was of more interest to Ash was Dorian later pointing out how expensive and inefficient the local technicians for the conference and talks were. They were famous, apparently, for overcharging and milking the monopoly they enjoyed as sole providers on the island.

'Honestly, Ash,' Dorian had said, 'you'd be better off bringing out your own technicians and flying in the equipment as well. It would work out better and cheaper, and you could leave some of the techie stuff out here for subsequent events. I realised that simple fact straight away at the Dockyard and we bought our own gear. Saved us a fortune.'

'I bet you're popular.'

'Dead right I am. That's why they kept mucking about with the mic during my talk and deliberately missed all the cues for the visuals.'

'Either you've really annoyed them, Dorian, or you rendered them dazed and confused, sending them off to sleep by talking in such detail about the development of Bermuda as a naval base.'

*   *   *

What was to prove even more significant to Ash, was Dorian's friendship with Doug Bonsall, a journalist on the Bermuda newspaper *The Royal Bugle.*

They'd been introduced to each other by Ash at the first event Dorian had participated in, as Doug was one of the handful of invited press attendees, and the sole local one.

Doug covered the event for the island's daily newspaper, not in truth because he found the subject matter fascinating, but for the simple reason that the opening address was given by a leading government figure – invariably one who was a close personal friend of Wallace Copthorne – and Doug was under a three-line whip from his editor to report on it.

Ash had liked Doug since first meeting him. With his black-rimmed glasses and slicked back dark hair, he looked like a cross between Clark Kent and Elvis Costello

– a combination of the earnestness of one and the indifference of the other, with extra lip curl thrown in if he didn't like what was being said to him.

Ash had tried to engage with Doug to get him onside for a big feature to promote the event, but he was having none of it, telling him that if Ashbury Events wanted coverage, they'd have to pay for advertorial.

Doug had preferred to ask Ash pesky questions like, 'What contact does Copthorne & Brookes have with the delegates? Is it just a selling excuse for the firm?' or, 'Do all delegates pay to attend or is it free places for the chosen?' and 'How much money does the conference bring to Bermuda, do you think, Mr Ash?'

Detecting a slight aggressive tone to the questions, Ash had tried to answer honestly by saying that there was nothing wrong with a firm promoting its brand with a bit of sponsorship and that there was no need to 'paper the house' with freebies as there were enough paying customers.

He'd managed to raise a wry smile from Doug by adding that, should the need arise to inflate the attendance levels, he would prefer to contemplate creating row upon row of dummy delegates, like the terracotta army buried with Qin Shi Huang, the first Emperor of China.

Ash had detected a kindred spirit behind the principled and investigative ambitions Doug displayed and had suggested to Dorian that it would be worthwhile cultivating him as a useful friend on the island, someone who could also promote the work Dorian did at the Dockyard.

The two of them found that they had much in common and their friendship had been cemented during the planning of what turned out to be 'The Captain John Smith Exhibition and Lecture Series', when Dorian contacted Doug to see what help *The Bugle* could give to its promotion.

At their first meeting to talk about it, Dorian had summarised for Doug – at length! – the Captain's importance as an explorer, colonial governor and New England Admiral. He'd given him a special reprint the Dockyard had just produced of one of Smith's books, originally published in 1624. This early gem of printing contained a section on the history of the Somers Isles, so called – as Dorian had helpfully pointed out – because of Sir George Somers, whose ship, the Sea Venture, had been wrecked in 1609 off Bermuda. Beginning to speak in footnotes, he'd detailed it as the inspiration for Shakespeare's play *The Tempest*, with Somers having thus founded Bermuda by accident. All of that happened when Captain Smith was Governor of Virginia, Dorian had patiently explained.

Doug, being the listening kind of reporter, had let Dorian labour through the facts – as only a historian can – before politely letting him know, 'Yes, I know quite a bit about him myself, having done a project on him as part of my degree course at St Francis Xavier University in Nova Scotia.' Ignoring Dorian's dropped jaw, Doug had continued, 'I can only agree it will make a fascinating exhibition if it's handled properly.'

Taken aback by the fact that the journalist had actually heard of Smith, they'd both burst out laughing as Dorian realised his own pretentiousness.

*   *   *

Further meetings to discuss how best to proceed inevitably led to the involvement of Gavin Boatwright as a sponsor, which resulted in a few late-night drinking sessions hosted at the Oxford Beaches hotel.

At one slightly more formal occasion, they were finalising the wording of some display boards to illustrate Captain Smith's management thoughts, published in 1626 in his book, *A Sea Grammar*, which outlined how to train young sailors for a life on board ship.

The group had just chosen two of the quotes they planned to use – direct from Smith's work – on the duties of officers. Dorian read them out:

'The Captain's charge is to command all, and tell the Master to what Port he will goe, or to what Height [latitude]

The Master and his Mates are to direct the course, and

command all the Sailers for steering, trimming and sailing the ship'

Gavin Boatwright said, 'They're job descriptions, that's what they are, and brilliantly succinct at that. That's a piece for your paper, Doug.'

'I could do a whole article on that aspect alone. Recently I did a feature on Nathaniel North – you know, Bermuda's infamous pirate son active around 1700 – showing how he split the spoils equally amongst the crew according to the pirate code. I could compare that with what John Smith's book says about sharing out of the profits resulting from the capture of a Man-of-War and contrast it with today's selfish chief executives.

Turning to the book, Doug added, 'Look! It says here: *"The Captain hath 9 Shares, The Master hath 7 Shares, The Mates hath 5 Shares, The Gunners hath 5 Shares, The Carpenter hath 5 shares, The Boatswaine hath 4 shares"* and so on.'

Gavin said, 'You're right, Doug. John Smith, from over three hundred years ago, puts the bosses of most modern companies to shame with their woolly thinking on roles and paltry profit-sharing rewards for their key staff.'

'You can say that again,' said Dorian. 'I gave a talk to a bank recently and when I asked each person to introduce themselves and outline their roles, none was very clear about what was expected of them.'

This struck a chord with Doug.

'That reminds me,' he said, 'during the last event run by your friend Ash, there was a guy called Wilkins who kept asking me exactly what some of the partners at Copthorne & Brookes did. I treated him to the local view that they did not do very much and even that, not very often. He said he was new to the island and asked me what I knew of the responsibilities of a few people he proceeded to name, some who worked in banks here on Bermuda, and others at local reinsurance companies. He wanted to know exactly what each of them did.'

'What on earth did you tell him?' Gavin asked.

'I was puzzled as to why he was asking me, a local newspaper hack, when he could have been asking other delegates or the people themselves. I mean isn't that what networking is about at these affairs?'

'Maybe he didn't want them to know he was asking,' Dorian said, 'or perhaps he wanted to get some local knowledge before meeting them.' He made a mental note that Ash would want to know about this, before adding, 'What did you say?'

'At first, I was non-committal about what I knew, just making general observations on their status and general standing on the island, but during the event, I did a bit of further research – not only on the people he'd named, but also into him.'

'This sounds intriguing,' prompted Gavin, 'do please

tell us what you discovered.'

'For a start, it was interesting that each of the people he named all went off to the same side meetings.'

'But that's pretty usual even from what I've observed,' said Dorian. 'They're probably members of the same insurance syndicate or some such, and I know they plan those get-togethers to happen at the same time as the conference – that's the reason they all come, so they can meet up and do some business as well as participate in the event.'

Gavin could see there was more to come, so held his hand up to shush Dorian and allow Doug, now warming to his subject, to continue.

'My research was helped by a little inside help from my mole at the JP Margeson bank. Apparently, the individuals named by Wilkins are part of some investment syndicate, not an insurance winding-up or run-off outfit. Mike Peters and Wallace Copthorne are the main men involved from Copthorne & Brookes. That same source also said that a bloke – and get this, it was Wilkins – had been into the bank to see one of the top brass. All staff received a memo straight after he left the building warning them off talking to him because he was from an outfit called Cogence Inc which is, apparently, an American corporate intelligence company and on the bank's blacklist. They were furious he'd evaded their screening procedures to even get a meeting inside their building. I think you should get Ash to do some digging in the UK about him, and Cogence for that matter, particularly as my own desk research didn't yield much.'

'Sounds fishy to me,' said Gavin. 'You could be on to some dodgy dealing there – you know what a murky world reinsurance is. You'd better tread carefully. I'd personally like to know more as I've got a rather large bone to pick with Copthorne & Brookes. They diddled an old friend of mine a few years back in what he was convinced was an investment scam and it caused him to have a serious heart attack from all the worry and stress. I wouldn't trust Peters further than I could throw him, incidentally, and as for his boss ... well ... Wallace Copthorne ... not for nothing is he considered a bit of a shark. That's why they call him the Bermuda Barracuda at the Yacht Club ... and the joke is that he thinks it's because of his fishing prowess. See if you can find any other dirt. One thing's for sure, you'll find something. Most professional firms these days seem to have greed as a silent partner.'

2.

LONDON

Ash wasn't surprised by Dorian's call from Bermuda to tell him about Edward Wilkins, because he'd already had a visit from the man himself.

Unannounced, he showed up at Ash's offices in Grosvenor Gardens late one afternoon. He apologised for not calling in advance, but said he had rather a delicate matter to discuss concerning the Bermuda conference and was there somewhere they could go to discuss it over a drink.

Ash had in fact spoken to Wilkins twice before – once in advance of the previous event when he'd telephoned to beg a small firm's discount to attend as a delegate. He liked Wilkins's cheek in asking, and, despite not being taken in by his pleas of poverty – his firm had a Mayfair office! – Ash gave him a special rate. Their second exchange was when Wilkins had introduced himself to Ash on Bermuda at the conference itself. He presented as a cocky south Londoner when he registered at the reception desk on the first morning. Clearly fancying himself as a rebel, he loudly told the staff that he was on a special list of attendees as he enjoyed a privileged VIP rate.

'I was pestered to attend for years by everyone in the reinsurance world,' he proudly announced to nobody in particular, and everyone in general.

No one listening believed that, of course, but he had some neck in trying it on.

Wilkins was bumptious and his pushiness could be witnessed at the coffee breaks in the way he went from group to group trying to get involved in networking. Chiefly, he seemed to end up on his own and was to be found chatting up the conference hostesses as often as not, and offering to take them out to dinner and show them the island. He had a go at each of them without any joy.

Despite the obvious rebuffs, he seemed irrepressible. Ash, being forty himself, put Wilkins at around the same age. With his thinning light brown hair, fleshy face and all-over-you manner, he had the air more of a moderately successful estate agent than a top-flight lawyer.

Despite these earlier exchanges at the Bermuda conference, Ash felt he should be polite when Wilkins turned up on spec at the office. He took him to the

Goring Hotel, just round the corner in Beeston Place. There, in the bar area, they grabbed two comfortable chairs next to the fireplace, right by one of the Goring's signature wooden sheep. Despite the relatively early hour, Wilkins spurned the offer of tea.

'No hot drinks after four-thirty,' was his rejoinder when asked what tea he would like.

As soon as the waiter came over to take their order, he said, 'I'll have a whisky and soda ... three fingers of whisky, please, and –'

'A glass of Sauvignon,' replied Ash.

'For my friend,' added Wilkins.

When the waiter walked away, Ash, irritated by the presumption of friendship, asked, 'What's this cloak and dagger, hush-hush stuff all about anyway?'

Looking around furtively, Wilkins leant forward. 'I just want you to know what sort of people you're involved with in this Bermuda conference of yours. Are you sure it's the right thing for your business? Reputation. Good-will. Brand image, and all that.'

Ash looked at Wilkins. He knew him to be pushy to the point of smarminess and didn't want to give him the satisfaction of appearing too eager to learn more. Naturally, he wanted to, and to ask for all the dirt on Copthorne & Brookes, but he didn't want to share his opinion of them with Wilkins and decided to play his cards close to his chest, merely raising his eyebrows to encourage more revelations. It was enough to give Wilkins the green light to press on with his conspiratorial whispers.

'They're crooks, you need to know that. Up to all kinds of unsavoury financial dealings. Surely you must know … perhaps you're involved … maybe I should just leave it at that.'

'Mr Wilkins –'

'Call me Eddie, please, not Edward, or Mr Wilkins. "Fast Eddie" to some, you may as well know. To be upfront, I haven't always been squeaky clean myself. Some tax schemes of mine, to be quite frank, have bordered on tax evasion rather than avoidance, but those buggers at Copthorne & Brookes are in a different league. Being no stranger myself to corporate delinquency, I'm now poacher turned gamekeeper, so to speak, because as well as my legal practice, I'm an associate of Cogence Inc, you know, the giant American corporate intelligence and research firm.'

'Why are you telling me this and not the authorities?'

'Look, I like you more than I like the powers that be, and, well, your company seems legit to me with a nice bunch of people working in it.'

Ash knew Wilkins tried it on with some of the female staff at the previous conference, so maybe the crude admiration he expressed for the employees he knew was genuine enough.

Ash shrugged, which Wilkins took as an invitation to continue.

'Did you know Mike Peters is a rogue and got into

big trouble in the UK? He nearly got struck off for fraud and he only avoided it by leaving for Canada where he requalified before heading down to Bermuda.'

'What kind of fraud?'

'Misuse of client funds for a start, but there was more to it than that. How he managed to slip out of the country without further sanction is a mystery to me. Friends in high places, I suppose. I know that his wife's father is an accountancy institute bigwig and her brother is high up in the Revenue. She wears the trousers in that relationship. And she's predatory, by the way. What an evil pair they make. I know about Peters because some of his past clients ended up as mine when I worked with Findlaters. We tried to start legal proceedings against him. Just as we were ready to proceed he did a flit, so it was a lost cause.'

Ash didn't have a particularly high opinion of Peters but at least he wasn't as bad as some of his other colleagues at Copthorne & Brookes. Admittedly he was lumbered with a very flirty wife, but that was hardly his fault. Was there more, Ash wondered? Wilkins must have read his thoughts, because he went on.

'Cogence want me to investigate Peters over an investment scam they've uncovered. I'm not surprised he's still involved in crooked practices. After all, a leopard never changes its spots. He's immoral too. You must know that Peters arranges prostitutes for any speakers who are interested. They fix it up at the speakers' cocktail party they host at that swanky house on Point Shares. That's divisive by the way. All the delegates who don't get invited are pissed off at the us-and-them apartheid they operate at what is meant to be an open event. We've ... sorry, most of us ... have paid enough, so we should get to meet the speakers at every opportunity and not let the partners of Copthorne & Brookes suck up to them exclusively at a private function so they can use it to further their own interests. Why do you allow that?'

'If you don't go to the party, how do you know about the prostitutes?'

'It's common knowledge but, specifically, one of the speakers last time was an old mate of mine. He was pretty appalled, let me tell you. And Peters has offered to do the same for some delegates. I wouldn't mind betting he does it to have some leverage over those who indulge. That's one way to build client relationships, I guess.'

'What are you suggesting I do about it? After all, these are adults we're talking about and unsavoury though it is, it does go on.'

'You should stop using Copthorne & Brookes. Simple as that. Use another firm or, better still, use a few other firms. Plenty would line up. It's such a prestigious event. I'd like to see them get their comeuppance. It's not just Peters. Take Wallace Copthorne – and I wish someone would. What kind of pompous ass is he? Breezing in and out like he owns the place, taking selected delegates out on his boat for some big game fishing. What a poseur. Did you see that disgusting article about him in the local paper when we were last there? He was pictured with umpteen stuffed animals in his home on Harbour Road – an obscene number of prize specimens of rare species and him sitting in the middle of them. Big game hunter? Complete shit more like!'

'You really don't like the firm, do you?' Ash couldn't help saying. 'But can I ask you one question?'

'Sure, fire away.'

'Do you want to come to next year's Bermuda conference?'

'Of course I do ... I need to attend for my legal practice's development and to observe Mike Peters and Wallace Copthorne. Any chance of the same discount?'

'Don't push your luck ... but if you'll agree to keep me informed of the progress of your investigations, I'll see what I can do. Leave it with me.'

'Great. I think we could help each other. If you need any more info at any stage, just let me know. I'll keep you posted – confidentially and strictly between us – of any interesting developments my end. '

'Another question – why hasn't Peters blacklisted you from attending? He presumably knows you've worked with disgruntled clients of his in the past?'

'No, fortunately. He seems to be in the dark about that. He only knew Findlaters represented his irate former clients. He never knew of my involvement. Now I'm a sole trader using my own name, he's not going to make the link. I've even spoken to him one-on-one and he obviously doesn't know me from Adam.

'It helped that I'm developing the captive insurance side of my own law practice, and, as I'm a lawyer, he doesn't see me as a competitor. Plus he smells money. We were talking about large brewers who find it cheaper to rebuild the few pubs that burn down each year than to pay to insure all of their properties.

'That is, of course, until they discovered they could set up their own offshore captive insurance companies on Bermuda and pay the tax-deductible insurance premiums effectively to themselves and accumulate the lot, tax-free.

'As soon as I told him I had a couple of brewing clients that owned a lot of pubs, he was practically eating out of my hand, telling me I must go to his house for cocktails and meet his wife. I ask you.'

Ash signalled to the waiter for the bill and thanked Wilkins for his time.

'Thanks, Edward … er … Eddie. If you've got anything in writing about Peters, that might be helpful.'

'Not sure I can let you have the stuff I've got without breaching client confidentiality, actually. Sorry! You'll just have to take my word for it. I'll keep in touch though. Let me know what you decide to do. Up to you what that is. Thanks for the drink.'

Ash sat, waiting to pay. He reflected on what Fast Eddie had told him. How much was down to Wilkins's resentment of Peters personally and of Copthorne &

Brookes by association? Was it professional envy or sour grapes at not being part of the inner circle? Was Wilkins jealous of those who were offered prostitutes when he wasn't? Where did Cogence fit in?

Ash knew the rumours about participants being entertained by women, so Wilkins's story held up on that score, even if Peters being involved in the pimping came as news.

But maybe there was another reason for Wilkins's antagonism towards Peters and his firm. Something didn't quite ring true about why Wilkins felt the burning need to share his views with Ash. What did it really matter to him? And how much could really be believed, even if it seemed perfectly plausible and fitted with Ash's own view of the sleaziness of the figures involved. Trouble was, that included Eddie himself.

He wished the meeting with Wilkins had taken place *after* Dorian had phoned to mention him rather than before, then he could have grilled Wilkins more about Cogence, as Doug's mole at JP Margeson had confirmed that Wilkins acted on their behalf. Maybe there was something in that after all. That added a further dimension.

*   *   *

Ash decided to have a meeting with his team, planning the next Bermuda conference scheduled for a little over a year's time.

Some of the attending staff were new to the event and, following Dorian's suggestion, he'd invited a technical guy – Ben Sanchez – who'd worked with them before, and had jumped at the chance to go to Bermuda.

After a preamble, describing the history of the event and why Bermuda was an important centre in the world of insurance and reinsurance, Ash got round to describing the painful procedure of working with Copthorne & Brookes. He stressed the sensitivities involved.

'It's a situation, a bit like an unhappy business partnership running a jointly owned enterprise, where each side can barely tolerate the other but recognises that they have to co-exist and work together, at least for the time being.'

'Why, exactly?' asked Dawn Grainger, who was going to be running the show for Ashbury Events now that Harriet Hall had left. Dawn, an old hand, was bright, didn't suffer fools gladly and had that easy air of authority that goes with being good at what you do and knowing it. Still fed up at having to run the Bermuda event that she'd been to only once, and with no proper handover from Harriet, she wanted to challenge how things had been run.

'Good question,' replied Ash, playing for time. 'For a start, each side claims to have come up with the idea. Copthorne & Brookes can't bring themselves to accept that we did, but at the start, we couldn't have done it without involving a firm like theirs. So, I suppose, maybe neither side feels they have absolute ownership rights or the right to leave the other and strike out their own.'

'What? You never entered into a written agreement?' Dawn was not impressed. Although new to the Bermuda Biennial she was a stickler for getting things tied down properly, legally, so that each party knew where they stood.

'Well, Harriet ran it and she was left to get on with it,' Ash said rather lamely.

'That's just the problem, isn't it? We don't know what loose verbal agreements she might have made or what she promised. And you know, don't you, that she's supposed to have had an affair with someone at Copthorne & Brookes? They'll be spitting feathers now that she's gone and baying for our blood.' Dawn sighed in frustration. Good at keeping her work and private life separate, she was exasperated by others who didn't. She loathed the fact that the events business was full of attractive people with messed-up relationships and was determined not to be one of them.

'This sounds like a fun event,' said Ben, bang on cue. 'Are you sure it's actually going to happen next year? Sounds like it's risky.'

'It *will* happen,' replied Ash. 'Both sides are doing well out of it. It's great prestige for Copthorne & Brookes, delivers a lot of new clients to them and, let's not forget, we're making pretty reasonable money out of it, so it is worth some pain. And, let's face it, Bermuda's a pretty good place to have to go to from time to time.'

'What's their slice of the action?' Ben asked.

'Not enough, according to the last letter I had.' Dawn always showed she was smart enough *not* to give an actual answer to a question, which allowed Ash to gloss over the detail Ben was looking for.

'It's a balancing act. They ask for more, but, in fact, as it's us taking the financial risk, we feel that taking a fat share of the profits is quite legitimate. Anyway, we haven't properly fallen out with them … yet.'

'Or improperly, if what you told me about Fast Eddie is true,' Ben stage-whispered to Dawn in an aside. Realising everyone had heard, he added, louder still, 'This Bermuda shindig is going to be interesting, that's for sure.'

Ash couldn't let Ben's reference go unacknowledged, especially as everyone laughed – showing that they all knew about it. Having told Dawn openly about Wilkins, he realised she'd passed it on – probably quite rightly – so that they'd all know exactly who they were dealing with. He decided to run with the common knowledge.

'What do you think of Edward Wilkins's accusations? Anyone?' Ash asked.

There were mutterings from the operations and marketing staff present before Dawn answered, almost on their behalf.

'We know from personal experience – all the women at the event do. Wilkins is a bit of a creep and makes a nuisance of himself. He seems to have a grudge against Mike Peters and is always bad-mouthing him, so that would point to taking what he says with a pinch of salt. But, Harriet was overheard on the phone one day – by everyone in the office – saying to one of her Sloaney friends, "You would not believe what actually happens on Bermuda, darling, it's like the last little whorehouse in Texas but with no taxes. Fnarr, fnarr, fnarr." Later, when you suggested that we offer a partners' programme for spouses run by your mate Dorian Miller, she was giggling afterwards and told me that it would never work for the simple reason that most speakers and delegates go on their own so they can have fun without partners cramping their style.'

Despite the smirks of those around the table, Ash tried, and was more or less successful, in getting the meeting back on track. They discussed what the proper planning priorities were and brainstormed some possible topics for the programme from those that had been suggested. They reviewed the timetable for the marketing campaign and talked about the costs and practicalities of flying out the technical equipment that would be needed now that Ben was involved.

He knew that these were the main elements involved in working towards the next Bermuda conference and they could get their teeth into those, but he didn't relish having to handle the unsavoury aspects that they were all now aware of.

3.

BERMUDA

Ash felt good to be back in his usual corner suite on the top floor of the older part of the Hamilton Princess Hotel. Awake early, still jet-lagged despite having broken his trip from London in New York, he ordered a pot of tea for himself. Once it had been delivered by room service, he opened the curtains before getting back into bed to drink it.

Comfortably arranged pillows gave Ash a feeling of total relaxation and he found it easy to sink back as if into history itself, and to contemplate the building's past life.

He loved the hotel, named in 1885 for Princess Louise, Queen Victoria's daughter, who visited Bermuda in 1883.

Mark Twain was a regular visitor, staying at the hotel right up to his death in 1910, and, drawn by the island's pink sands, considered it 'the right country for a jaded man to loaf in'.

Ian Fleming, when a naval officer, lodged at the hotel during World War Two when it became an important British counterintelligence outpost. The enormous fish tanks that once graced the hotel's bar were, allegedly, the inspiration for the predator-filled aquarium in *Dr No*.

What inspired Ash even more was the fact that the spy chief Sir William Stephenson, a prototype James Bond by all accounts, occupied a penthouse suite at the Princess for a time after the war. Code-named 'Intrepid', he oversaw British intelligence operations in the Western Hemisphere.

Ash fantasised that it was the same suite as he was now lounging so lazily in, drinking his morning tea. He couldn't help wondering what role he might have played in the war. How would he have measured up to the challenges?

Bermuda, he knew, was an important mid-Atlantic clearing-house for British Intelligence and the centre of the censorship service routinely opening thousands of letters carried between Europe – especially spy-ridden Lisbon – and the Americas, by ship and Flying Clipper.

'Trappers' – the nickname for the team of code-breakers – operated out of the hotel with the job of reading and analysing enemy communication at high speed, especially electronic interceptions of German submarine signals.

In what was then known as the 'Bletchley in the tropics', Ash realised that his role would probably have been more with the mail sifters in the basement of the Hamilton Princess than at the sharp end of intelligence operations. He realised he was more ingenuous than ingenious, and much more introvert than intrepid.

What he'd learnt in New York had shown him that. He still hoped that it wouldn't change the way he thought of Bermuda, a place he was realising was still full of secrets and undercover activity. Who knew how it would all pan out?

*　　*　　*

Sitting up, he could see across the waters of the harbour and he looked out expectantly, having heard the long blast of a ship's horn. He guessed there was a big liner making its way across the Great Sound to glide through Two Rock Passage and into Hamilton Harbour. He waited for it to drift past his window as it made its way towards the dock. It was close enough to see the passengers lining the upper decks, all of them pointing and waving at nobody in particular.

These, he knew, would be Americans in the main who

embarked at New York and would soon be disgorged at No. 1 Shed, the pink terminal for cruise passengers. They would go en masse to buy up whatever they could from the main shops: china from AS Cooper & Son, clothing from HA & E Smith's – extra large sizes available – or maybe hand-baked assorted cookies from Trimingham's gift boutique for when they got peckish between their huge meals.

Ash decided to give Front Street a miss that morning – to avoid the influx of tourists – and hire a moped to scoot over as arranged to see Dorian at the Dockyard. It was most unlikely that any of the new arrivals would go and visit something as interesting as that, and he made a call to confirm lunch with his friend.

Ash showered and dressed and went down for breakfast – pancakes and maple syrup – surrounded mostly by Americans. Although a British territory, the influence of the US, Bermuda's closest landmass, was all-pervading and the clash of cultures didn't give it a cutting edge so much as trap the island in the past, giving it a 'middle-aged' feel, which was part of its charm.

After breakfast, he fixed up a few meetings for later that day and into the next and then lost no time in getting hold of a moped from Astwood Cycles at the front of the hotel.

Despite car hire not being permitted to visitors, Ash liked the independence of having his own transport on the island and set off for a slow ride round the harbour to make his way to the Royal Naval Dockyard, along that part of the island that looked, on the map, like a scorpion's tail.

It was a beautiful day. With Jimmy Buffet playing on his headphones, fittingly singing about 'expatriated Americans … running from the IRS', Ash rode through Hamilton along Front Street and was cheered to catch sight of Johnny Barnes, Bermuda's 'Mr Happy', still smiling after finishing his stint of greeting and waving at the traffic on Crow Lane roundabout. Ash envied him his sunny, good-natured and simple approach to life.

Taking Harbour Road, Ash took in the pretty pastel-coloured houses with their distinctive white, stepped, rainwater-catching roofs. Most had gardens with a profusion of dusty pink oleander, tropical hibiscus and palmetto trees set against the blue waters of the harbour.

Further on his journey, along Middle Road, before crossing Somerset Bridge, Ash looked out for Robert Stigwood's house at Wreck Hill – his tax exile home for more than a decade up to 1992.

From there, the journey was through Bermuda's answer to the Florida Keys, before reaching the far end of the island where Dorian lived and worked. It was hard not to envy his life when compared to the daily commute Ash had to make across London to an office in Victoria.

He consoled himself with the thought that it all might be a little too perfect, and would, perhaps, get claustrophobic after a while.

Ash laughed as he realised that humans can rationalise anything if they put their mind to it and can even talk themselves out of living in paradise.

He started thinking about how much he really knew about the island. Did he know it at all?

As he rode his moped on the quiet roads, passing the odd pink bus, he felt he was in some kind of sub-tropical Toytown, idyllic in almost every way if you discounted the minor irritants of Copthorne & Brookes, the Sly and Gobbo partnership of evil goblins he had to deal with.

*　　　*　　　*

Ash had arranged to meet up with Dorian at the Frog and Onion at the Dockyard.

When he joined his host inside the old-fashioned pub, he found he'd already been ordered a steaming bowl of fish chowder because it was promptly delivered to their table as soon as he sat down and exchanged greetings.

'Blimey, Dorian, are you in a rush to get rid of me?'

'Don't take it the wrong way, but … yes! I've got a session this afternoon with a school group. Sorry. I can't be late for that and I thought we could meet up again later as well and you could buy me dinner.'

'Sure,' said Ash, 'I'd be happy to treat you. Why don't you see if Doug's around and we could make a night of it.'

'OK, I will, and in that case, I'll pay for this,' Dorian joked. 'My expenses can run to a couple of soups, I think. By the way, don't forget to lace it with local black rum and the sherry peppers sauce that are in those little jugs in front of you. They'll really lift this soup and turn it into an unforgettable experience.'

'How long have I got you for?' asked Ash.

'Forty minutes or so, if that's all right?' replied Dorian. I'll let you know what I've got planned for the spouse programme at next year's event, if you like.'

Encouraged by Ash nodding his head whilst eating his soup, Dorian continued.

'I thought that the main experience should be a ferry trip out here to the Dockyard after they've breakfasted, with coffee on arrival and then a brief lecture on the history of Bermuda, segueing into an introduction to the naval importance of this "Gibraltar of the West". I'd follow that up with a short tour of the Dockyard itself, you know, the Ordnance buildings, the Victualling Yard, the Cooperage, the Commissioner's House and a last stop at the museum. That would then lead us into a light lunch followed by an hour or so for the shops – the Commercial Director insists on that – and a ferry would take them back to the Princess mid-afternoon.'

'How many can you cope with?'

'Ideally around thirty, and that means the staff here

can accommodate them for lunch.'

'Sounds good! I doubt we'll have more than that number of participants, box office draw though you undoubtedly are, Dorian. Do you have any more suggestions for trips on other days?'

'Really? That should be enough, shouldn't it, what with the other socials you lay on for them? If you like, I could do notes on places like the Botanical Gardens, St George's and the Aquarium – you know, some things that they should try and see during their stay on the island – and leave them to organise it themselves if they want to.'

'OK. Can you give me a puff on the Dockyard trip in good time for us to include it in the brochure. You can then let me have a few pages of tourist suggestions well in advance of the conference so that we can include them in the handouts.'

'Will do.'

'Now ... you can tell me what you've been up to and what the local gossip is.'

'I'll leave Doug to talk about that. He's been investigating certain financial dealings that might be of interest to you as they involve your friends at Copthorne & Brookes.'

'Oh, no!'

'Why do you say that? I think it's all very intriguing and stuff you should know about.'

'Sorry, but it's just that it fits with a few things I heard on my stopover in Manhattan on my way here. Things

I'd really rather not know, but I suppose will have to be faced up to.'

'Tell me about New York – that sounds much more interesting than what goes on here.'

'Well, I was hoping for a relaxing time there, seeing a few potential speakers and linking up with some old mates, but things took a bit of a nasty turn when I met a guy who turned out to be with the FBI.'

'How did that come about?'

'Incidentally, this must be kept strictly confidential. Not a word to anyone – anyone at all on the island ... or off it, for that matter. I still haven't processed it myself and I really shouldn't be saying anything as I've been told to keep it to myself.'

'Of course! You have my word.'

'So, there I was thinking I was meeting a boring moneyman that we were trying to sign up to speak on corporate capital problems. One of our lawyer contacts had put me onto a bloke who was part of the Lehman Brothers insurance team. His name is Tony Merino. So far, so good. But, he then turned up for our arranged meeting at the Royalton where I was staying – very sophisticated hotel by the way – with a shifty-looking guy who turned out, cutting a long story short, to be an FBI agent.

'Tony Merino first introduced him as "Carey" who he'd done some work with from time to time. He said this Carey chap was also keen on getting involved with the conference. They had me explaining how the

Bermuda event had started, who controlled it, who chose the programme and the speakers – lots of detailed questions that I answered as best I could without giving away all the secrets. I thought they were just interested in the background. How naïve am I?

'Later, this Carey tells me, "By the way, the name's Carey ... *Merino.*" Turns out they were brothers. He then told me straight out that he was FBI and had a particular interest on Bermuda as part of a major investigation.'

'What's that about?'

'I'd been suspicious because, right from the start, it seemed that the Lehman guy would speak for us, yes, but *only* if this new chap was given a free place at the event, like an observer, but under an assumed name. When I innocently said that I would probably have to clear it with Copthorne & Brookes, they quickly disabused me of even entertaining that notion. They could see I was a bit startled at this, so Carey dropped his shiftiness and that's when he told me he was FBI. It was like a B movie, especially when he told me rather than asked me, "You'll have another drink and then we can talk some more, Mr Ash," in a thick New Jersey accent with more than a bit of menace. I've never wanted to be back in London as much as I did at that point.'

'Sounds exciting to me. I can't imagine anything like that happening here,' said Dorian. 'What direction did the talk take then?'

'We got some more drinks. We were all on Old

Fashioneds by then and the whiskey fortunately calmed me a bit. He started by saying that Bermuda may seem a kosher regime, properly regulated and all that, but that hadn't stopped it from being used by organised crime. He gave me a history lesson taking in the Mob of the fifties and sixties, money laundering down the ages, as well as dodgy real estate deals and hotel funding operations used to disguise the proceeds of crime.

'He laid into us limeys saying it was all very well the Brits pretending to uphold the rule of law, but at the same time maintaining a grip on important secrecy jurisdictions like Bermuda and the Cayman Islands. He knew of supposedly reputable and professional Bermudian law and accountancy practices that turned a blind eye to the origin of huge sums of money. Top criminal financial brains had nosed these firms out, he said, and regularly used them to hide their ill-gotten gains. And he talked so much about Ponzi schemes that I had to ask him what they were.'

Dorian was looking blank, so Ash explained.

'They're pyramid selling scams where money from new investors is used to pay out profits to the early investors, robbing Peter to pay Paul until the whole thing collapses. He reckons that he's onto a big scheme, centred on Bermuda, that involves Copthorne & Brookes, can you believe.

'He grilled me for what seemed like ages to see if I knew more. Fortunately he could see I was completely in the dark, but I don't mind telling you the whole experience has left me rattled. They want my cooperation and I think I'm going to have to take some legal advice when I get back to London.

'I had to say I'd use Tony Merino as a speaker and allow his brother to attend as a delegate, but I don't actually know what to do about them. However, the weirdest thing is, this Carey guy then offered me a whole range of insurance regulators from different states who could speak for us, including some names we've been trying to get for years. Seems like he knows them all and wants to have a few with him on Bermuda.

'With the next outing for the conference nearly a year away, I said I couldn't see what good that would be to his live investigation. He waved my objection aside saying they had a lot of leads they were following up which would take time and he wanted to "catch 'em big *and* catch 'em all".

'Apparently, with some insurance and financial scams, it can take years to unravel what's going on, especially if several states of the US and countries overseas are involved in the investigation. *Plus*, in this case, he wanted to give Copthorne & Brookes enough rope to hang themselves.

'He wants it to play out a while longer without Mike Peters, Wallace Copthorne and other known suspects realising that they're under investigation. That way, with any luck, they'll implicate themselves and other participants in their activities. It made me wonder if he actually had much to go on at all at the moment.

'I tried to suggest there was little point in him or any of his people coming to the conference and he rather alarmingly said he wanted that to be the occasion when everything came together. He knew that various critical meetings would take place at the time of the event when he thought key persons of interest would incriminate themselves – he wanted them to be caught in the act. He needs to use *our* conference to gather the final pieces of evidence as conclusive proof of malpractice, fraud, criminal conspiracy and all the rest of it.

'I suddenly felt I was in deep with him and the FBI, *and* with no way out. I don't like it. I feel like jacking it all in and letting the conference disappear up its own ... I should have realised earlier that they were related as both have the same look – almost identical Italian features but with Tony the tanned banker and Carey the pasty-faced cop.'

Dorian took it all in and said, 'I can tell it's a bit of shock. Very unpleasant! Maybe you should put Carey Merino in touch with Doug. He too is investigating various nefarious networks of crooked professionals here on Bermuda.'

'I felt guilty not mentioning that Eddie Wilkins guy. I think I told you that I'd already met up with him when you rang to say he'd been nosing around Doug, but I don't think it's fair to land anyone else with this FBI thing without their permission.'

'Doug is different though, right? You can tell him about the FBI, surely?' said Dorian.

'How can I mention *them* to Doug without breaking their confidence? I've got the same problem with Wilkins. I suppose I could tell the FBI about them both, especially with Wilkins being involved with Cogence, which is bound to be on their radar. I suppose I could just mention the interest Wilkins *and* Doug have shown in all this and leave it to the FBI to decide whether to contact either, or both, of them. Wilkins I don't particularly care about, but it could land Doug in trouble, so I'll have to think about how to handle him. I don't think his bosses on *The Bugle* want him ferreting out stuff that would reflect badly on Bermuda or suddenly getting involved with the FBI.'

'No, they wouldn't. They spiked one early, fairly innocent piece he submitted and Doug got the message. He keeps it quiet from them. He's working on a book and he feeds stuff to some worldwide forum of journalists looking at tax avoidance and financial scams involving plutocrats from around the world.'

'It makes you question the status of Bermuda, doesn't it? OK, so GDP is high and they boast about that. But its favourable tax, confidentiality and untraceability regime is what drives it. Being used as a tax haven for corporate entities that hide illegitimate activities can't be right.'

'I think Doug wrestles with his conscience a lot. On

the one hand, he's a loyal Bermudian and proud of the island and its heritage, but on the other he finds the way the island profits so much from the shady world of finance to be rather unsavoury.'

'We should just stay out of it. It's not our axe to grind, is it? Financial affairs can be a bit boring. I'd rather not get involved in the scary stuff.'

'How can you say that? It sounds fascinating to me. Gives you a story to tell, "My brush with the FBI", or you could write a novel about it,' said Dorian.

'Very funny. Anyway, enough of all that. It's too depressing. Tell me. How's your love life?'

Ash was keen to stop himself talking about financial skulduggery anymore and regretted saying anything at all before he'd properly thought out what it all meant and how he should play it.

Dorian also looked relieved to change the subject.

'Life out here is pretty tame, you know, once you've discounted the kind of expat bed-swapping that goes on and the drunken flirting – and worse – at the parties of the snobby local bigwigs.'

'Does that mean you've been pursued all over the island by Fiona Peters?'

'I was. It got worse as she kept turning up at the Dock-yard or ringing me. I felt I was being stalked and found it quite intimidating. Frightening even. There were times I was tempted, but she's trouble that one.

'She even pitched up late one night at my room at

Oxford Beaches. Luckily I was sitting out on the verandah with Gavin, my regular nightcap buddy.

'She actually ignored me and started flirting with him, fortunately, as if they'd unfinished business to attend to. Eventually he said he'd take her off to put her in a cab. Funny thing was, a cab did leave with her in, but not until six the following morning, just as I was setting off for my early morning run. That's what goes on here.'

'So Gavin's a bit of a dark horse, is he? From what you've said, I thought he was fairly straight-laced.'

'Gavin? No. He's a wealthy guy from way back and has a reputation for being a bit of a ladies' man. He also happens to like nautical stuff so, to me, he's a good sort, but I was told that money and women have been his other main obsessions.'

'What about him and Mike Peters? Does *he* know about Gavin and his wife?'

'There's certainly no love lost between them. I saw them once in the same room at one of our fundraisers, and Gavin made a point of leaving as soon as Mike Peters and his missus arrived, kissing her ostentatiously on the way out.'

'Find out more about Gavin and Fiona, will you? That might be useful.'

'One evening Gavin told Doug and I that he hated Peters and didn't trust him or Copthorne & Brookes. Something about a mate of his being swindled or something.'

'I think you've swerved a bullet with Mrs Peters, but shame there's no special friend for you out here.'

'I didn't say there wasn't, did I? Actually, I'm seeing someone who's been working on secondment at *The Bugle*. She's been drafted in because she did some work for a couple of top newspapers in London and now helps *The Bugle* on the technical side, computerising their editorial and typesetting procedures.'

'Where did you meet?'

'Don't laugh, but we met at The Devil's Hole Aquarium.'

'What on earth were you both doing there?'

'It was an introductory talk on the sea life of Bermuda. Did you know there are over six hundred and fifty species of fish in these waters – bonefish, pompano, grey snapper, yellow and black fin tuna, cumberjack, wahoo –'

'Stop, stop! Don't tell me this is your latest obsession, Dorian? And no, you're not doing a lecture on it at the conference.'

'Well, as luck would have it, she was more on my wavelength, pardon the pun, than you are. We bonded over seeing angelfish, green turtles and moray eels. She's introduced me to scuba and we go diving at the weekends to the local wrecks. In the water she looks just like Jacqueline Bisset did in the film *The Deep* – which was, interestingly enough, Ash, filmed here on Bermuda.'

'Really? Tell me more ... no, don't. But, you can tell me more about her.'

'No need – you'll meet her tonight if you like. I can

see if she's free.'

'Yes, why not? So long as you don't talk about fish all night, other than to choose one to eat. And having her with us might at least mean that we don't have to talk about the world of financial shenanigans with Doug.'

'Too late! She's already involved in all that. She's put Doug in touch with a team of investigative journalists at one of the Sunday papers in the UK and he's doing some work with them on tax havens and money laundering – on a strictly anonymous basis and with no byline, of course. She finds all that stuff fascinating.'

'Oh, God, Dorian, I shouldn't have shot my mouth off about the FBI.'

'No, don't worry. I'll keep mum. I won't tell Bee about it.'

'Bee?'

'Beatrice actually, so, not surprisingly, she prefers to be knows as Bee.'

'Bee what?'

'Bee ... don't laugh ... Goode'.

'Is she?'

'I'm a gentleman, Ash.'

'It sounds ... bloody good to me. Are you bewitched, bothered and bewildered ... maybe even a little bit *be-sotted*?'

'As if I'm going to tell you. We get on well, let's put it like that.'

'OK. That's great. I'm looking forward to meeting her.

Where shall we go? I was thinking Elbow Beach as I've got to talk to them about the gala dinner arrangements. If I tell them I'm eating there tonight with friends, they might do a deal or throw in some wine. But remember, not a dicky bird about the FBI to Bee … or to Doug.'

'Roger that!'

'Dorian! Are you talking about Bee again?'

4.

BERMUDA

Ash and Dorian went their separate ways after lunch, with Ash feeling stupid for oversharing with his friend and possibly putting him in an awkward position with both his new girlfriend and with Doug, his main buddy on the island.

Ash set off on his moped and called into the Port Royal Golf Club to fix the arrangements for the golf tournament that would be part of the social activities at the next conference. He then rode along Middle Road and onto Harbour Road, taking a detour past the area in Warwick where Eugene O'Neill had once had a winter home in the 1920s, a house called Spithead. Ash knew that the house next door, Spithead Lodge, had belonged to Noel Coward who spent some time there in the 1950s when he wasn't in Jamaica, but could still continue to enjoy his status as a tax exile.

Ash stopped to take a look at the property. He managed to catch a glimpse of the house surrounded by oleanders and vast flamboyants in its gardens that edged the bright turquoise water of the Little Sound.

He admired the location with its view out to Darrell's Island, the early quarantine centre for ships arriving at Bermuda and the site of the island's first airport, where Pan Am and Imperial Airways seaplanes first landed in 1938.

There was, away to the right and in the distance across the water, a view of Hamilton. What a place to live, he thought. It even had what looked like its own classic wooden Chris-Craft 20' Riviera boat moored at the bottom of the garden. Ash wondered who lived in the house now and how much it was worth.

He momentarily fancied buying a boat and setting himself up as tour guide to the houses of the rich and famous. What with Stigwood's house, O'Neill's, Coward's, Ross Perot's, Mrs Kirk Douglas's family hotel – Ariel Sands – and a few others, maybe a tour like that would work. He could promote it as a side attraction to any of the large conferences that were held in the Hamilton or Southampton Princess hotels. Plus, if it were offered to all the other tourists ... and the large cruise ships –

Wait! He pulled himself out of his daydream. It dawned on him that it was a pretty naff idea, pandering to the worst sort of people's prurient interests – people ... like him, he realised. No, he couldn't do that. Ghastly!

Another business plan holed below the waterline before it was even launched. Leave the idea for somebody else. 'And over to the left, we have the fabulous house of X, the world-famous celebrity who came to Bermuda as a tax exile and lived an idyllic life of pampered luxury...'

But were they happy? Ash asked himself.

Yes, probably!

*   *   *

Back in Hamilton, before returning to the hotel, Ash picked up some melatonin from the US-stocked drug store where you could legally buy it over the counter, thinking it might help him get the sleep he was craving.

He then stopped at Miles Market to buy himself a bottle of Gosling's Black Seal rum, a few cans of Barritt's Bermuda ginger beer and a large packet of Pepperidge Farm Goldfish crackers so that he could have his own Dark 'n' Stormies and snacks on the hotel balcony, without having to pay through the nose for room service.

Having parked his moped at the hotel, freshened up in his room and made a few calls, including one to the Elbow Beach banqueting manager, Ash headed back into Hamilton.

Strolling along Pitts Bay Road, he admired the lavish fountains of the Bacardi head office – where he could imagine a team of accountants mixing a mean, low-tax corporate cocktail for the shareholders. He then walked past some enviably attractive waterside office buildings and the elegant Waterloo House Hotel. He had to force himself to think about his impending meeting with Copthorne & Brookes and he tried to plan how he should play it.

Keep it normal, he told himself, especially given that they don't know what's in store for them at the event itself.

They'll be aggressive, rude and moany about us, snooty about last year's event, wishing it drew more bookings and demanding of a bigger cut. Plus I'll get stick about Harriet. Generally, they'll be posing as the top dogs in the relationship and expect me to lap up whatever macho snidery they can dish out. I'll take a bit of banter, but –

What was I ever thinking, running anything with this lot? Have I no shame or pride? Am I just interested in the money like most people who come to Bermuda? Perish the thought!

The meeting was as bad as he feared. He was kept waiting in reception, long enough to read on the notice boards the names of the many offshore companies that had their registered offices in the poky building that housed Copthorne & Brookes. Nearly all of them were likely to be brass-plate companies, that's all. He knew of one US multinational that had a one-man booking office in Hamilton and no local sales on the island. What a farce. It was mainly so that the companies concerned could claim that management and control was based on Bermuda to get residency and enjoy its low tax regime. A sham, in other words.

The poor visual appearance and state of the offices further offended Ash, given that it was such a wealthy firm. Perhaps the partners wanted clients to think their accountants couldn't afford swanky offices, thereby proving that the fees they were paying were perfectly reasonable. As if!

It was more likely to be because Copthorne & Brookes had no taste or style. That was borne out by the old battered furniture in the general office that he noticed on his way through to the firm's boardroom, which only appeared elegant in contrast.

Ash took in the sight of the long-suffering clerks who were shuffling papers, sitting in sections like the rowers in a Moorish galley. Some looked up at Ash as he passed as if pleading to be rescued. He knew how they felt and would try his best to avoid joining their slavish ranks by not kowtowing to their bosses.

*   *   *

He was paraded into what looked like a partners' meeting, a dozen or so older men – it's always men, isn't it, he thought – sitting in their, no doubt, customary places. They all stood in mock politeness as he entered, each one dressed identically in blazers, shirts and ties and wearing Bermuda shorts, long socks and black brogues to complete an almost Ealing Comedy look. Or was it more sinister than that – resembling as they did the overgrown schoolboys of a Dennis Potter play?

Ash was gestured to a seat that was at the far end of the table, facing the day's chairman, Wallace Copthorne, who was first up on his feet – no doubt flexing his authority as presiding partner.

'Say hello, everyone, to none other than ... Mr Ashbury Events himself. We'll overlook, shall we, gentlemen, that he's still not wearing Bermuda shorts to come to meetings with us when he's on the island. But, he is an out-of-towner and likes to show it, so we'll say no more about it.'

They all laughed, as if to say, he's not one of us and never will be.

Nice welcome, thanks.

Copthorne held court again.

'We were just saying that we could do with more people at the next event. Our American friends think the marketing could be a lot slicker. What do you say to that, Mr Ash?'

'Attendance was higher than previous years and the

feedback we got from the delegates was very complimentary, as usual,' was all Ash managed in reply, but he sensed a burst of adrenalin firing him up. He realised he'd have to fight to keep his cool.

Copthorne ignored the reply.

'Of course, the programme itself was very strong and that's what really pulls them in. We *all* know that. But *we* do that for you, don't we? What we have to ask ourselves is this: what can *you* do for us to grow this event into a major international fixture, like Baden-Baden, for example? That's *our* ambition and it should be yours.'

Ash was expecting this gripe and guessed it would be used to put him on the spot. Whilst Copthorne was speaking, Ash secretly hoped that the FBI would burst through the doors and arrest the whole bloody lot of them.

Instead, he settled himself in for his ritual humiliation with Copthorne grandstanding for his partners. Ash knew the best defence was careful deflection of the insults and artful demolition of false arguments. Inwardly he knew he could take whatever was thrown at him, knowing the next conference now had a bigger purpose.

As the partners all studied him to see how he would deal with Copthorne's point, Ash replied, 'Well, you have to recognise that this is a Copthorne & Brookes-sponsored event and that puts off a lot of people who work with other firms of accountants. You have to see it in context, which makes the attendance we do get quite remarkable. That's what's different from the reinsurance event at Baden-Baden.'

'The Americans think you can't get it right,' piped up Mike Peters. 'Take the badges you give out to delegates. Our US senior insurance partner thinks they're too small to read. At *our* events, there's room to show the nicknames that wearers are usually known by. Unless all the detail is on the badge, you may as well not bother. If you can't get the little things right, then the Americans don't trust you with the big things.'

Here we go again. Ash had heard this rather petty complaint before and knew the Yanks wanted big badges for delegates with names like Henry 'Hank' Bluster III, Blunt, Bluff & Flannel.

Too bored by the question even to answer it rudely, Ash rolled with the punch saying, 'We can look at that aspect, if that really is at the very top of your list of problems.'

That needled Peters who came back with, 'Getting down to the nitty-gritty, as all the costs must now be known, can you tell us our profit share from last year's event?'

'Forty thousand dollars,' Ash replied, and gasps went round the table.

Thrown by the partners thinking this was a good result, Copthorne said, 'Before we get carried away, let's remember that's barely enough to cover our internal costs – what with the party, the entertaining we do for our overseas clients and the travelling expenses of a lot of the speakers that we pay for. I bet Ashbury Events make a profit from the event. We don't.'

Ash said, calmly he thought, 'Look, we all have additional overheads and other costs to net off from our respective profit shares. Can I point out, respectfully, and stop me if I'm teaching my grandmother to suck eggs, but … you're accountants … surely you know that the costs you incur are part of your practice development. To find the true return on what you spend, you'd have to compute the growth in client base that results from your participation in events like ours, estimate the additional fees earned as a result and then deduct the costs. On that test, I'm pretty sure you get a good payback.'

This didn't go down very well with any of the men around the table.

'Hell, Mr Ash,' Copthorne responded. 'It's our event. We want it bigger and better and we need to know that Ashbury Events are the firm to entrust with our intellectual property.'

This got Ash's goat and he threw caution to the wind. 'You bandy the word "our" about quite a lot, Mr Copthorne, but I'd just like to remind you that, actually, the whole event was my idea in the first place and, for better or worse, I approached you to see if you'd like to work with us on developing it. Isn't that so, Mr Brookes?'

Ash turned to the white-haired and patrician Selwyn

Brookes, the now semi-retired Senior Partner who sat to one side of Copthorne. Ash was pleased Brookes was there and that once and for all he could publicly get proper acknowledgement of where the idea for the event had actually originated.

All eyes were on old Mr Brookes, who Ash knew to be an altogether more benign figure than Copthorne and had the added advantage of sounding like Jimmy Stewart.

'Well, Mr Ash, what you say is quite correct. I can remember our initial contact, as a matter of fact, when you made your first visit to Bermuda to discuss your conference idea. And, if I may observe, I think it has always gone well and our firm has benefited from its association with the event. It's helped our growth and helped to raise our international profile considerably. The Americans love the event and, naturally enough, the chance it gives them to come here to Bermuda. My old friend the Prime Minister sees it as a perfect showcase for the financial services the island offers. We should continue to move forward in a spirit of cooperation. But that's just my view.'

That swung the moral advantage to Ash and he saw that Copthorne and Peters were pissed off by Brookes, and what they saw as his guileless observations. Ash imagined they would be inventing ways to pension off old Selwyn as soon as possible.

Copthorne was then onto the offensive straight away.

'If we're talking about the past, can I just ask about

Harriet Hall? You know we enjoyed working with her. She *was* the conference as far as we were concerned, and we knew where we were with her. Frankly, things have gone downhill since she left, Mr Ash, no offence. We weren't consulted about her going and it's changed the whole thing for the worse as far as we can tell.'

Ash was ready for this one.

'Other than out of politeness, I don't see why I have to explain why we felt we had to part company with Harriet any more than I would expect you to keep me advised of any relevant changes in personnel at Copthorne & Brookes, even of people working on the event. I would naturally expect that continuity would be assured by the professional way staff changes would be handled by your firm. And that's what you should expect from us. After all, your business relationship is with Ashbury Events and that's continuing. You can't really be saying that your relationship was with Harriet Hall, can you?'

Ash knew that this was hitting a nerve and he expected a tough comeback from Copthorne who, instead, just stared at him before replying.

'You may think that you are able to get off the hook, Mr Ash, but like any of the blue marlin I have caught off Bermuda, no fish is too big or too clever not to be caught eventually.'

Peters saw that Copthorne was going nowhere with his fishing analogy and stepped in to spear Ash on his boss's behalf.

'One thing the Americans are concerned about' – it was strange how Peters always blamed the Yanks, thought Ash – 'is whether Ashbury Events have the best reputation. They ask whether you have the right standing in the insurance world for us, one that actually enhances our own by being involved with you. Their concern is that our image could suffer by being tied to yours. What do you say to that?'

Tempted as he was to mention the FBI, Ash found himself limply replying, 'We may not be the biggest, but we are one of the best, in my opinion. I would say that, wouldn't I, but we have a reputation for honesty, integrity and straight dealing that other companies in our business don't. I'd say we're a good firm to be associated with. Naturally, we assume the same of Copthorne & Brookes ... that you don't sail too close to the wind or risk any harm to your own goodwill. Fear of being tainted by association cuts both ways and so far neither side has had any problems on that score.'

By this point, Wallace Copthorne had clearly had quite enough of Ash for one day.

'If you don't mind, Mr Ash, we have some important partners' business to attend to as we have been blessed with a rare visit from Mr Brookes, so I'm afraid I'm going to ask you to carry on discussions with Mike in a separate meeting room.'

Ash stood, thanked them for their time and left, to the clear relief of all, it seemed.

'You were lucky that Wallace didn't blow a gasket in there, Ash,' Peters said as they made their way to another office. He seemed anxious to smooth things over and was very polite and friendly, stressing how important it was that they both worked hard, and together, to keep things on an even keel and not rock the boat. He didn't realise this made him seem like a two-faced git after all that smarming and sucking up to Copthorne in the boardroom.

They discussed and agreed a lot of detail in the follow-up session. 'We both need this event to work,' said Peters at one point, 'and I'll do all I can to make sure it does. Please come to me with any problems and I'll try to smooth things over. I can handle Wallace. Leave him to me.'

Ash struggled to take Peters, or anything he said, seriously, not least because he tucked his shirt into his underpants. He was a sycophant and smarmy with it. Prematurely grey, he arrogantly leant back in his desk chair with his arms folded as if to say, I'm the one really in charge here.

Peters – who Ash thought had started to look like a clone of Wallace Copthorne, in the fattish and well-fed sense – got particularly excited when told that Ash had secured Tony Merino from Lehman Brothers, no less, as a key speaker.

'That's a coup. You should have announced that in the meeting. We've been dying to get in with Lehman

Brothers for years – we all feel they're our kind of firm, birds of a feather, you could say.'

Ash could already hear Peters claiming credit for it later as the partners enjoyed their usual post-work sundowners at the Royal Bermuda Yacht Club at Point Pleasant.

*   *   *

As he walked back to the hotel, Ash ran through the highlights – for want of a better word – of the meeting, mentally preparing the notes he'd have to write up when he got back to his room. It had been unpleasant to live through. To relive it in his mind, as he walked back along Pitts Bay Road, was even worse.

Ash couldn't help thinking that Peters had seemed a bit too desperate and totally out of character in his attempt to appease him in their one-to-one meeting after the awfulness of the session with the partners. Peters had even passed up the chance to twist the knife. Why?

As he neared the hotel, Ash realised that so much must be riding on the next event for Peters that he simply *had* to make sure it would go ahead.

*　　　*　　　*

No sooner had he arrived back in his room than the phone rang. It was Mike Peters.

'I forgot to ask you just now whether you still see that awful journalist from *The Bugle*, you know the one I mean, Doug Bonsall.'

'I do, yes, from time to time,' replied Ash. 'Why?'

'You're a friend of his, aren't you?'

'I like to think so.'

'Well, he asks a lot of questions – keep him away from the event in future. I'd rather you didn't discuss it, or any other Copthorne & Brookes business with him, if you don't mind.'

'That's a bit difficult, not least because *he's* the one *The Bugle* insists on sending to cover the event as he's so well known in government circles. I'm trying to get him *more* involved if anything, writing bigger features about the conference.'

'Don't. That's all.'

'Why? What's he done?'

'He's always sniffing around. Upsetting people with intrusive questions.'

'That's what journalists do. Don't let it upset you.'

'I'll tell you what also annoys me about him. As he takes his own photos for his columns, he's always there snapping away at this or that social event. Once, he deliberately contrived to get my wife in shot in the background, looking as if she's getting off with some bloke. It's almost like he was making a point and it didn't go unnoticed amongst our friends. It's none of his bloody business what Fiona and I do in our relationship. That's why I don't want you to encourage him to think he's got any influence. Treat him like the guttersnipe he is. Thanks and goodbye.'

Peters slammed the phone down, which gave Ash even more to think about – the evening with Dorian, Bee and Doug at Elbow Beach was going to be very interesting.

5.

BERMUDA

The finest run of sandy beaches on Bermuda lies on the south side and the one at the Elbow Beach Hotel was Ash's favourite. He'd arranged to meet the banqueting manager at the hotel's beachfront Café Lido, which was down the hill from the main hotel building. To get to it, he had to pass various attractive bungalow rooms dotted around the landscaped gardens that flowed down to the shore.

He then spent a pleasant hour or so running through menus and arrangements, agreeing likely numbers and costs. Ash explained he was entertaining a few close friends after the meeting, making a point of mentioning exactly who they were, and he was pleased to be told that the hotel would cover their bill.

As evening came and he was left to await the arrival

of his friends, Ash strolled along the beach barefoot. He listened to the evening chorus of whistling tree frogs and chirping crickets, overdubbed by the swooshing ocean, a combination that was Ash's favourite Bermudian soundtrack.

He was calmly sitting at a table on the beachfront terrace enjoying a Papa Doble – the Hemingway daquiri – when Doug arrived in a bit of a state.

'That Peters bastard has just tried to run me off the road. I swear he did. I nearly came off the bike as he drove me into the side of the road. I swerved all over the place and only just managed to avoid going straight into a tree.'

'Are you sure, Doug?'

'Course I'm bloody sure. You should have seen his grinning face and the smirk I got from his tarty wife. Both of them were laughing and waving as they sped past and zoomed off.'

'Where was this?'

'On Stowe Hill as you come up and over onto South Road.'

'Let's get you a drink, Doug.'

As a waiter came into view, Doug ordered a Rum Swizzle and Ash asked, 'Why do you think it was on purpose?'

'First, they *must* have followed me as that isn't the logical way to come here from Hamilton – you'd use Trimingham Road. Secondly, there were some roadworks with temporary lights. They flicked to red as I approached, but I shot through and, although their car must have been further back, it still ignored the red light. They came screaming up behind me and then overtook just as we left the roadworks.'

'Don't you think they might have just been doing the same as you – jumping the lights, but getting too close, and then waving to apologise when they saw you were OK?'

'Christ, Ash, were you born yesterday? They would have been happier to see me end up in a heap on the side of the road.'

'Yes, but how would they have known you'd be riding over from Hamilton to Elbow Beach at the precise time you were?'

'Because they must have been waiting for me outside *The Bugle*'s office in Par-La-Ville Road, and, what's more, I've seen them there before.'

'It's near the Copthorne & Brookes offices, isn't it, so could it just be coincidence?'

'You're being a bit obtuse tonight, Ash.'

'Not really, I'm trying to calm you down enough to talk this through rationally.'

'Calm down? Are you joking?'

'Well, just to stoke your conspiracy theory even more, I had a call from Peters this afternoon and he sounded mightily pissed off with you and your "snooping around" as he put it. He even said you'd deliberately put a picture in the paper that showed his wife with another man. Maybe he *is* annoyed enough – although I can hardly believe it – to drive you off the road.'

'See. It all makes sense.'

'OK, OK. Perhaps your version of events is right, but I was hoping it wasn't the case.'

This seemed to relax Doug – at least he was being believed – and they both ordered another round of drinks. Ash was disappointed at this latest turn of events and knew the evening was going to be dominated by it unless he was careful.

*   *   *

Dorian and Bee's arrival lightened the tone just in time, and in recounting his scrape to them, Doug managed to find the humour and bravado that can come with the retelling of a tale, especially in front of an attractive couple.

Ash could see why Dorian was smitten – Bee was a very pretty brunette with incredibly alert eyes that seemed to be fixed only on her partner. She was very relaxed and her presence seemed to cheer Doug up. The group buzzed through various topics of conversation with a lot of laughter.

Unsurprisingly, they all enjoyed their starters. When told the evening was on the house, they all – including Ash – proceeded to choose the fresh Maine lobster with a champagne cocktail sauce served in a coconut shell – the most expensive starter on the menu. Oh well, he thought, only slightly shamefacedly, why not? When in Rome...

Ash was determined to steer any conversation in a light-hearted direction, at one point even telling them about his idea for a tour of the island focusing on the houses of the rich and famous.

Doug said he thought it was too frivolous and a bit downmarket, but Bee loved the idea and offered one of her own.

'I did a course on the botanical delights of Bermuda when I first arrived and I'd love to do a guided tour to show off my new knowledge of Bermudiana, bird of paradise, frangipani, freesias, ginger, kumquat, loquat, oleander, passionflower –'

When she paused for breath, Doug said, 'That's all in alphabetical order too!'

'I can see why you and Dorian get on so well,' said Ash, 'you're just like him.'

'Nerdy?' suggested Dorian.

'No ... no. You both love to learn all you can about a subject. Nothing wrong with that.'

'I think you're politely trying to say that we're fellow obsessives,' replied Dorian. 'And, just to prove it, forget about plants and millionaires, I've thought of offering a lecture at the next event based on the time John Lennon spent on Bermuda. I've looked into how he came to be here, writing the songs that featured on what turned out be his last album.'

Even the arrival of their main courses didn't stop Dorian explaining his idea in greater detail. As they settled into scallops, pan-fried soft-shell crab, and escalope of veal, the exploits of the ex-Beatle provided another interlude of light relief.

'Did you know that when he came here in 1980, he hadn't written a song for five years? Then, in the couple of months he was on Bermuda, he wrote twenty-five great songs including, "(Just Like) Starting Over", "Watching the Wheels" and "Woman",' said Dorian.

'And did you know that the album, when it came out, was called *Double Fantasy,* which is the name of a freesia Lennon saw in the Bermuda Botanical Gardens?' Bee said, before adding, 'Sorry ... no more plants, I promise.'

'But did *you* know,' Doug said, 'that I was there at the Rock Lobster on Front Street dancing along with everyone else to the B-52s, on the very night in 1980 that Lennon came in? I saw him. I really saw him. How about that? And, the next day, apparently, he picked up his guitar and started writing songs again. No wonder he loved Bermuda.'

'Where did he live when he was here?' asked Ash.

'Ah, this is where my research comes in,' said Dorian.

' He took a house a couple of miles out of Hamilton in Fairylands – that area that takes in Point Shares and Mill Shares Roads. It's like a private estate, which all the wealthy merchants in the Hamilton of old made their own, but are now, incidentally, occupied by a good few, or a bad few, partners of Copthorne & Brookes. The house Lennon chose was called Undercliff and was right by the water. You can see it from the road, but it looks even better from a boat.'

'What did he like about Bermuda?' Bee put her hand proudly on Dorian's to encourage him to talk more. She clearly liked his voice. Doug caught Ash's eye and winked, as Dorian continued.

'He hadn't been in Britain for nine years or so, and because of that, perhaps the Britishness of Bermuda reso-nated with him. Can you imagine the contrast between this island's calmness and the rush of New York? It's sad to think that four months after he left here in July 1980 he was dead – and so soon after getting his head together to recover his song-writing mojo, right here on Bermuda.'

'Sounds like a good lecture,' said Ash.

'You could even play some of the tracks from the album,' Bee suggested. 'I'd certainly go to a talk like that.'

Doug, Ash could tell, was perhaps thinking that love's young dream was proving a bit much, because over coffee he said, 'Somebody should really talk about the *real* Bermuda, the side that the visitors don't see. There's more political and commercial cronyism than you'd think. Some islanders lack trust in public institutions and allege corruption in the way infrastructure contracts are handled. And, it's not a liberal place, you know. Gays and minorities don't have an easy time even now, and it was quite segregated until the sixties. There's been recent unrest too, with racial tension not exactly unknown, like when the Governor, Richard Sharples, and his aide were assassinated in 1973 by the Black Beret Cadre, a militant Bermudian Black Power group. I don't suppose your delegates would like to focus on that, Ash, would they?'

'That would come as a nasty surprise, for sure,' Ash replied. 'I think people see the island as a wealthy and stable society where you can walk around freely and not fear for your safety.'

'That's the problem,' said Doug, warming to his theme. 'Everyone who visits the place sees it as made up of the haves ... and the have-yachts. That's it. They think *everybody* who lives here is loaded. But the reality is a bit different. It's a curious mix of old family snobbishness and incredible wealth, some of it in the hands of families that dominate the political scene. But there is the other side of the tracks, like the area on the North Shore side of the island, up and over from the Governor's residence on Langton Hill.'

'Best we don't explore that with the delegates, and leave it to you to write about, eh, Doug,' Dorian ventured.

*   *   *

They stayed for an extra nightcap – on the house, of course – and Doug and Bee joined forces, getting very excited about exposing corruption on the island. Ash and Dorian, not wishing to get too involved, questioned the role short-term visitors should have in that task.

'Leave it to Doug to get to the bottom of all the financial intrigue,' Dorian said to Bee at one point, seeing the look of exasperation on Ash's face.

'That's a head-in-the-sand attitude, Dorian, and I'm disappointed in you,' Bee replied. 'It's an international problem, with investors being ripped off from America and Europe. If I can help expose the abuses, I'm going to.'

That was her unequivocal response when Doug outlined what he'd recently discovered about something he called the 'Bermuda Bond', a dubious scheme that Mike Peters, Wallace Copthorne and others on the island were known to be involved in.

'There's a link between the Bermuda Bond and their own captive reinsurance company, CaBRe. Money from investors flows in, out, *and* between both concerns as well as to and from companies owned by the wives of Wallace Copthorne and Mike Peters.'

Doug explained that he had a source at JP Margeson, the main Bermudian bank, who had personally handled the relevant accounts. When this mole of his had tried to flag some suspicious activity with his superiors, he'd been transferred sideways – which always means downwards – to work on domestic lending only.

'This is why Peters is concerned about me,' Doug told them. 'This business about his wife's mugshot being caught in my photos is baloney. He knows I'm onto him.'

The turning point in the conversation at Café Lido came when Ash, in an unguarded moment, said, 'I think if it's an international problem, it's better left to the international enforcement agencies who, no doubt, are already looking at it.'

When Doug and Bee snorted in derision at this apparent cop-out, Ash added, 'I mean ... leave it to the FBI, for example.'

Dorian looked into his glass at the mention of the FBI, relieved that he wasn't the one who'd let the cat out of the bag.

Of course, after that, Ash was pressed into explaining what he meant and was persuaded to give details of his experiences both with Carey Merino in New York *and* with Eddie Wilkins in London. Difficult though it was to wriggle out of why he hadn't said more a lot earlier, Ash managed to assuage both Doug's outrage at what he felt was a breach of trust and Bee's astonishment at his 'flagrant duplicity' as she put it. Ash tried to say he didn't want to involve them with the FBI, and had been trying to respect the confidentialities of all involved.

Dorian was quiet throughout Ash's embarrassed justi-
fication for his actions. Bee noticed that and, inevitably,
she asked him straight out, 'Did you know all about this,
Dorian?' In reply, he merely suggested they took a walk
on the beach.

Whilst they were gone, Ash apologised profusely to
Doug, who eventually shrugged it off, saying, 'These are
tricky matters and I know you've got business dealings
with Copthorne & Brookes, so I can see you have to
be careful in how you handle it. But you've got to put
your trust in someone, sometime, Ash. And that goes for
Dorian as well. No wonder Bee is pissed off with him.'

When Dorian and Bee returned, they'd clearly been
arguing and matters were only resolved when, as they
took their seats, Doug calmly said, 'Look I respect people
trying to protect confidentiality. That's all Ash was doing
for me *and* for the FBI. Listen Bee, poor Dorian here was
only respecting the trust he and Ash have between them.
As a journalist, I know the importance of not betraying
a confidence.'

Ash then obtained Doug's permission to mention him
to the FBI and they all agreed to pool what information
came their way from whatever source, including Wilkins,
and swore allegiance to each other and the greater cause.

'Honesty amongst friends is a greater force for good
than honour amongst thieves,' Doug said, but Bee was
more theatrical about it.

'Let's all put our right hand on top of each other's in

the middle of the table to mark us working together. We have a bond – *our* Bermuda Bond – one you can't buy and sell ... a real friendship. We can't throw that away.'

Dorian looked at Bee. Maybe he was getting a bit too fond of this girl. 'I read somewhere,' he said, 'that loyalty should be reserved for those we love rather than those we serve.'

'Amen to that,' Doug added, and he, Bee and Ash looked at Dorian and smiled.

*   *   *

Ash realised on his sobering ride back that the evening had probably been a mistake. What had they let themselves in for, he wondered, as he weaved his way back to the Hamilton Princess.

6.

BERMUDA

The first thing Doug did after his night at Elbow Beach was call his old school friend, Scott Roberts, an inspector in the Organized and Economic Crime unit of the Bermuda Police Service.

'I need to see you, Scott. Urgently, if possible.'

'Wopnin?'

Irritated, as Scott knew he would be, by his friend's constant habit of using local slang, Doug replied, as he always did: 'What's happened, I think you mean, is that someone tried to kill me last night by driving me off the road.'

'That's a bit of a jump even for you, Doug, isn't it? You can't go round accusing every bad driver of attempted murder.'

'There's more to it than that, obviously. That's why I need to see you.'

'OK. I'll drop by *The Bugle* within the hour. We can grab a coffee and you can tell me wopnin. Then, I'll try and prevent you acting or talking out of order.'

'*Stop de madness*, you mean, surely, Scott?'

'You said it, Dougie, not me. See you later.'

Scott was used to Doug trading on their friendship to obtain info for his newspaper articles and assumed he needed a friendly policeman to talk to once again. In the early days, their regular contact caused a few raised eyebrows amongst his superior officers, until they realised that Scott always came back with more than he gave away. Doug proved to be a useful source of valuable leads that helped the force with their enquiries. Their respective bosses trusted the pair of them not to spill too many beans either way.

It was strange, therefore, that only a few minutes after Doug's call, Scott was summoned into his chief's office.

*   *   *

Over their coffee, Scott was wary because he now knew that someone 'on high' was complaining about Doug undermining the standing of the financial services sector on Bermuda by asking impertinent questions. 'He's some kind of commie bastard' was the phrase used.

Scott's boss had told him that he should perhaps cool his relationship with Doug for a while, or it might affect his career prospects. Although he didn't believe the accusations himself, he had warned Scott that a witch-hunt could be taking shape. 'Be careful,' he'd said, 'in your dealings with Doug. I've got your back but the Assistant Commissioner who's behind the allegations is on friendly terms with Mike Peters and, let's say, even friendlier terms with his wife. Neither of them has a good word to say for Doug.'

This gave a normally sceptical Scott even more cause to try and play down Doug's accusations against Mike and Fiona Peters. He hinted at the conversation he'd had with his boss before giving his reaction to Doug's story of what had happened the previous evening as he rode over to Elbow Beach.

'Look, I'm not saying I don't believe you, Doug. It's just that there is bugger all we can do about it. Even if I fed this into the department concerned, there's no proof. Nothing. And, as I've just told you, we're going to have to be more careful in our dealings – for the time being anyway.'

'In other words, Scott, what you're saying is this: even if I get killed, you might not look into it.'

'Come off it, Doug. You can see there's nothing to go

on yet. You're going to have to put together a pretty strong case against Peters, and for more than just road rage if you want us to go after him. He's got influential friends in the force, more's the pity for you. Between you and me, even my chief thinks the Assistant Commissioner is very sweet on Mrs Peters and the talk of the canteen is that the AC attends swingers' parties hosted by Mike Peters. One Hamilton drug dealer squealed about seeing him there when he revealed who he supplied.'

'Why is he still in post then?'

'Well, the AC denied the accusation, of course, and got very indignant about it. He insisted on confronting the dealer who later – surprise, surprise – claimed he'd made it all up. Very convenient. Doug, if you do have to investigate Peters and his dodgy deals, for God's sake be careful.'

PART TWO

BERMUDA & LONDON, SPRING 1995

7.

DOUG

Doug had grown to resent his general dogsbody status as a journalist. He aspired to greater things than interviewing the victims of sunglasses heists, or reporting on the Premier of Bermuda attending the opening of an envelope.

He'd tried his best to craft interesting features on Omega Gold Cup Yacht Racing and World Rugby Classics, despite having zero interest in sport. He'd interviewed visiting captains of cruise ships, hotel managers and various celebrity visitors and had given his best shot at turning out Pulitzer award-winning stories, but, whenever he offered to do in-depth articles on anything important or worthwhile, he was fobbed off. Local interest were two words he'd come to hate.

Despite the discouragement, he didn't stop suggesting

ideas for the paper. Feeling inspired one day, he rang his editor and said he wanted to do a series profiling the heads of the major law and accountancy firms on the island and, for good measure, a regular slot on the higher echelons of the Bermuda Police. 'How's that for local interest?' he asked.

His editor laughed and told him instead to go and interview members of a ladies' book club who would be meeting over tea that afternoon at the Hamilton Princess.

Doug was still fuming about being demeaned as a journalist, and worrying about his downmarket reputation, when he walked into the hotel's residents lounge later in the day and found the only likely table of women at the far end of the very large and very pink formal room.

He went through the process of taking their names and affiliations, laboriously at first, until their book choice of Nick Hornby's *High Fidelity* revealed that they were a lively bunch, and his hopes were raised that it would not be an entirely wasted journey.

Quickly realising that you can't judge a book by its cover, Doug discovered that one of the group was also a writer herself. Linda LaFong turned out to be the author of the critically mauled *Love on Bermuda*, and the ex-wife of Gavin Boatwright, the multi-millionaire owner of the Oxford Beaches hotel who was Dorian's patron.

Gently he teased out of them all, and from Linda in particular, some fascinating snippets of financial and sexual scandal going back several years. So that's what book clubs are about, he thought, as he made discreet notes.

Linda casually dripped revelations about Gavin and several other prominent men friends of hers over the years, and the others tried to compete, all seemingly forgetting they were talking to a journalist.

Doug realised that they must all think him a real dingbat who just reported on school sports days, golf club tournaments and book clubs. It didn't appear to matter to them what they revealed in their gossip, until it dawned on them, momentarily, when he stood up to leave.

'I hope you won't be reporting on our loose talk, Mr Bonsall?' said a panicky Linda.

'Don't worry, none of this will make it into the paper,' he reassuringly replied.

Doug could hardly make it down fast enough to the Colony Pub in the hotel lobby where he ordered a beer and sat up at the bar to go through his notes.

Gavin Boatwright involved with the New York mafia? Never! Handling hot money for the Mob from extortion rackets and investing it all for them in hotels in the Caribbean? Plausible? Yes, and so too was his possible link with a drugs operation involving the ocean research unit he generously sponsored. Boats offshore for supposed legitimate purposes being used to ship drugs in and out. Why not?

And what about the empty shell of the derelict hotel at St Catherine's beach? Can it really have been built with the proceeds of organised crime and drug cartels as one of the women had suggested? Was it a monument to money laundering?

There was much giggling when the sex parties run by Mike and Fiona Peters had been mentioned. Linda said they were the cause of her divorce as Gavin's fling with Mrs Peters had started at the one and only wife-swapping party she had foolishly been gulled into attending.

Another woman had then chipped in that it was well known that Peters ran what he called an elite investment club, drawn from men who'd been to his soirées and who were more or less blackmailed into putting up funds to participate in the investments offered.

*   *   *

Doug continued on with his investigations into Mike Peters and Wallace Copthorne.

When the FBI's Carey Merino got in touch, thanks to Ash's intervention, to say he was flying down to Bermuda to take a look around, Doug knew that he had much to tell him.

Following an afternoon phone call, they met that evening at Rum Runners, a favourite of Doug's on Front

Street. Its ornate wrought-iron balcony reminded him of the French Quarter in New Orleans, and the great jazz pilgrimage he'd made there as a teenager.

Rum Runners was where Doug often met Dorian, who liked the gigantic nautical figurehead that dominated the restaurant's entrance, but he hoped he wouldn't bump into his friend whilst he was meeting with the FBI.

Over a Rum Swizzle, Merino said, 'Before we start, let's agree that we'll respect each other's confidentiality whilst sharing information on subjects of mutual interest'.

They ordered their food and got down to business.

'Assume I know nothing and tell me everything you can about Mike Peters,' was Merino's opening gambit.

'Peters is a junior partner, with aspirations – or delusions – of grandeur, who operates from his professional base within the accountancy firm of Copthorne & Brookes. He and his wife are well known on the island for their wild parties and open relationship. They have friends in high places in the police, the government and the financial services authorities.'

'So, handle with care?'

'Exactly,' said Doug. 'The accountancy side is a bit of a front, in my opinion, and he seems more interested in getting investors into his Bermuda Bond fund and that needs much deeper investigation –'

'Go on.'

'From what I've learnt from a contact at the bank of JP Margeson, investors are invited to put money into the

Bond, which then invests in another company owned by Peters and Wallace Copthorne – the big cheese in the partnership. The company concerned is a reinsurance business called CaBRe – Copthorne & Brookes Reinsurance to give it its full name. They are both experts in this area, so clearly wanted their own vehicle to cash in on market demand. Money flows from the Bond to CaBRe and back again and the sole directors are Peters and Copthorne and their wives. I've got copies of documentation showing large loans between the companies and fees to the wives.'

'This Bermuda Bond – how do they get their investors, do you think?'

'According to some, they use blackmail to a certain extent, having compromised high net worth individuals at their sex parties. The pay off is that the victims are "invited" to invest in the Bond and it's an offer they can't refuse.'

'Do you know this for a fact?'

'I know that at first they relied on parties at their home, then, when an old contact of Peters and Copthorne turned up very recently on Bermuda, they resurrected the idea of an upmarket brothel.'

'Who's the old contact?'

'It's a woman called Harriet Hall, who used to work with Peters on the conference that Ashbury Events run every couple of years.'

'OK. That squares the circle for me.'

'Peters and Hall think they're a bit too clever for the rest of us. They opened offices for a business they call Queen of the East, which specialises in importing Chinese artefacts, but actually it's a brothel copying the name of an infamous house of ill repute from the past that featured in a book by a local author, John Weatherill.'

'What's the role of this Harriet Hall woman?'

'She organises the girls – sorry, shop assistants – and all the parties. She keeps the files on the punters they attract and presumably gives the info to Peters. And, of course, as a front, she handles all the importing and selling of their Chinese products.'

'Does Peters know you're on to him?'

'I think so. I thought he just saw me as an awkward local busybody, but now that he's tried to bump me off –'

'Bump you off? How do you mean?'

'Some time back, he and his wife deliberately tried to drive me off the road when I was on my moped and I ended up in the ditch. The latest attempt was much worse.'

'What happened?'

'I was tricked, I later realised, into going to an address on the north side of the island. I received a phone call at the office from a supposed drug dealer, refusing to give his name but claiming he wanted to "tell all" to *The Bugle.* He spun some spiel about finding God, wanting to go straight and come clean. I arrived at the address I'd been given at the appointed hour of ten in the evening. It was a dark and deserted road, but I thought no more about it. I parked up, but as soon as I got out of the car I was sapped on the head by someone who appeared from nowhere.'

'Wow, buddy, this sounds serious.'

'Coming to, I ached all over and was bleeding from facial wounds. I'd been beaten up in other words.'

'And were you robbed?'

'Yes, of my wallet and my work camera. And my bag was taken, but fortunately it only contained a blank pad of paper. I more or less crawled to the door of the house and just about managed to knock on the front door. It was opened by an elderly woman who, after hearing what had happened, kindly bathed my face and called the police.'

'What did the police do?'

'To date, nothing. They think I was duped into a mugging and with no witnesses they've got nothing to go on.'

'What did you tell them?'

'I told them I thought Peters was behind both attacks, but he's convinced them that I'm a crank with a personal grievance against him. Even my friend in the local police has told me to drop it.'

'Who's your friend in the Bermuda Police?'

'Scott Roberts – a bright guy who works in the Organised and Economic Crime unit.'

'Have you told him what you've told me?'

'Some of it, but he's already pointed out that Peters

has protection at the top and that any allegations I make would have to be fully documented before he'd even take a proper look.'

'Is he honest and above board?'

'I'd bet my life on it. And his Chief Inspector too – the block would be higher up.'

'Have you mentioned me to them?'

'No. I thought it best to keep that to myself.'

'That's good. This visit of mine is kind of unofficial. If I needed their cooperation, I'd have to go through the right channels and I'm not ready for that yet.'

'I won't say anything to anybody – apart from the friends who already know about you from Ash.'

'Who, for chrissake?'

'Dorian Miller, who's an academic with the Naval Dockyard, for one, and his girlfriend Beatrice Goode who's an IT wizard and helps with some of my financial research. But I haven't said anything about you to my mole in JP Margeson.'

'Tell me about this bank connection of yours. Who is he?'

'He was a senior manager in the international department, but was sidelined to handle domestic business when he tried to flag concerns about certain suspicious transactions. He told me the bank has a sophisticated infrastructure and a very interesting client base dealing with major corporations and wealthy individuals. They act as a conduit or a service provider. He really understands their systems and he knows more than they think about operations in places like the Cayman Islands and Hong Kong.'

Doug was doing most of the talking up to this point because he only had to contend with a plate of seafood brochette and crab legs, whereas Carey Merino was eating all that *plus* a giant sirloin, a combination plate of huge proportions.

'What else you got for me,' Merino asked, as he was finishing up.

'What? Food or facts?' asked Doug.

'Not food, Doug – I admit defeat. Let's have a coffee.'

'I'd urge you to follow up with my friend Beatrice Goode. You should definitely see her.'

'Why's that?'

'Bee – that's what she prefers to be called – is, like I've said, romantically linked with Dorian, and because of her computer prowess, she came to Bermuda to work at my newspaper on its IT systems. It turns out her skills on database management are greatly in demand on the island. She's picked up quite a few consultancies, including one with the law firm Lemon, Lockhart & White, who handle all the legal work for Copthorne & Brookes as well as the personal affairs of Mike Peters and Wallace Copthorne. She's got a stash of info which could prove to be highly damaging.'

'Where would I find her?'

Doug passed a large envelope over to Merino.

'You'll find a summary there of what I know and some contact names and addresses of individuals and companies, including Bee's details.'

Over coffee and local rum, Carey Merino then gave the bare bones of the FBI case.

'I can't say too much at this stage, Doug. I know you've been straight with me, but our investigations are running in a great many different directions. We already suspect that the Bermuda Bond is a major scam, but need to get hold of bank records here on Bermuda before we can act to guarantee a watertight case. The authorities don't really play ball with us if they think our enquiries are speculative. The Bond has a sales force in Florida preying on the rich retirees who want to park their money offshore. We've an undercover agent working down south in Miami for the Bermuda Bond Investment Fund and we're close to a breakthrough.

'We've got insurance and reinsurance experts working in various states across the US to piece together an intricate jigsaw of Bermuda companies, all linked to CaBRe. The money involved is scary and what you say about the flows between the Bond and CaBRe points to fraud on a gigantic scale. It doesn't surprise me that Peters might be resorting to violence to make you keep your beak out of his affairs. You might need protection, buddy. Until you get it, keep a low profile. Try and put Peters at his ease. Be nice to the guy. And, here's a tip, be even nicer to his wife. Put them off the scent whilst we work on the facts and evidence to nail them.

'If you think of anything else, you'll find me at The Rosedon, across the road from the Princess – more private. I'm checked in under my own name, by the way.'

*   *   *

What Doug didn't tell Carey Merino is that he and Bee were working closely together on assembling a great mass of material that revealed the complex affairs of a good many international rogues, Bermuda-based rotters and shell company ownership structures which would be dynamite in the hands of the FBI, the IRS, or any one of a thousand different countries' tax authorities. Bee could tell him if she wanted to.

Doug had worked with Bee during many late nights and, inevitably, they'd crossed over from friendship to a more intimate relationship. Doug was wracked with guilt, not alleviated by Bee saying, 'We're in a *Jules et Jim* situation, Doug. That's all. Let's tell Dorian. I'm sure he'll be fine about it.' Doug thought otherwise and counselled discretion for the time being.

The other matter Doug did not mention was the book club's revelations and Linda LaFong's finger pointing at

Gavin Boatwright's mafia connections. That could be an ex-wife's wild accusation and he needed to check it out before embarrassing or betraying someone else he regarded as a friend.

8.

BEE

Bee was enjoying her time on Bermuda. She liked Dorian and his straightforward approach to life. She knew where she was with him. Doug was different; more edgy, more anarchic and a rebel at heart.

This is what Beatrice Goode fancied herself to be. Always had. Rules, what were they? 'For the guidance of the wise and the obedience of fools.' She applied that maxim to her own life and interpreted everything in her favour.

Take her latest conundrum. How could she carry on a relationship with both Dorian and his friend Doug? 'One at a time,' had been her father's advice when he'd found out she was two-timing one of her teenage boyfriends. But what did he know?

She was perhaps duplicitous – someone had called

her that once – but it came so easily to her that she didn't lose sleep over it. If 'what they don't know won't hurt them' was applied to the men in her life, then, hey, that was an OK philosophy to live by, wasn't it?

She didn't set out to deceive, not really. It was just that opportunity presented itself, so why not? She liked the Oscar Wilde saying that he could 'resist everything except temptation'. This made her feel quite normal in her approach to relationships.

'It's not a rehearsal,' she said to herself in the mirror every morning, never challenging her thinking, just doing what suited her in the moment.

When Doug and she were working late one night, she had kissed him and one thing led to another. She'd stayed overnight at his apartment. The wine helped to relax them both and she liked him. He was good looking and interesting to talk to. It seemed the natural thing to do.

She liked Doug's journalist image. He had some great stories. She admired his ambition. He and Dorian were, if anything, two sides of the same coin: one a historian, one a journalist; one investigating the past, the other the present. They both find me desirable, she thought, so what's not to like?

Doug seemed to be uncomfortable with cheating on his friend Dorian. Why? If it didn't bother Bee, why should he let it get to him? He hadn't liked the idea of telling Dorian. He wasn't relaxed about that at all.

Bee had always been secretive. That was her modus

operandi and she was careful not to take anyone into her own circle of trust. If Doug wanted to keep it from Dorian, that actually played to her strength – keeping it zipped, well, mostly.

This latest work of hers with *The Bugle* had led to some lucrative contracts. She could handle the project at the newspaper comfortably and, as news of her computer nous spread, she was given access to the fascinating and hidden worlds behind the average display screen sitting on the desk of a professional lawyer, for example.

When Lemon, Lockhart & White called her in and offered her a consultancy to sort out their electronic filing system, she leapt at the chance.

For a start, the senior partner, Raymond White, was quite flirty with her. Promising, she thought, let's see where that leads. It clearly blinded him, as he gave her all the access codes she needed to go anywhere in their system and look at everything. The network architecture was insecure and servers were not segmented from client databases. It was hardly hacking if you were given access, was it? Working from the inside felt less criminal to Bee.

What's more, she found thousands of files and recognised a lot of the names. It was no problem to take electronic copies and hide the trail.

Doug was astounded with what Bee showed him and they worked together on what they christened the Bermuda Papers: attorney-client information on oligarchs, dictators, kleptocrats in public office, CEOs, big companies, small companies, and shell companies from Russia, China, the Middle East, Hong Kong, the Philippines, the Cayman Islands, Gibraltar, Cyprus and the Channel Islands.

Seemingly, there were thousands of individuals and companies, all hiding behind complicated corporate structures and secret shareholdings and proxies. So much dirt, in fact, that Doug told Bee to park it for a time whilst they worked out how to use it for the best.

One morning, Doug phoned Bee and told her about his meeting with the FBI guy who was on Bermuda and might be in touch with her. 'How exciting!' she said, 'I've never met a real-life FBI agent. That'll be a first!'

*   *   *

He didn't disappoint her. A tough guy, obviously, but charming in his own way, Carey Merino had quite a smile, she decided, when they met for lunch on the dockside terrace of Waterloo House.

Playing on his Italian heritage, perhaps, he ordered linguine with shrimp whilst complaining of the sky-high prices. She insisted on a glass of champagne to accompany her crab tartare and toasted 'success in all our endeavours'.

Bee noticed some wariness from the other side of the table throughout the lunch. She, naturally, sold to him her unparalleled access to information sources on Bermuda and enthusiastically spoke of her shared interest with Doug in exposing personal and corporate greed. But that didn't seem to be good enough for the FBI man.

'Who do you really work for?'

'Myself, of course, who else matters? I'm a consultant and I decide which clients to get involved with. I'm not an employee. Naturally, I sign non-disclosure contracts, so I'm careful about that, but some things are bigger than pieces of paper, don't you think?'

'Like what?'

'Well, you tell me what you're investigating and I'll tell you what I might have access to. Then you'll have to convince me that it would be right to provide you with certain materials, as a whistleblower might – more of a leak than an act of theft.'

'Doug has already given me the lowdown on certain key people on Bermuda that are persons of interest to us. Can you help provide documents and contracts that relate to *their* activities and offer more than Doug has already done?'

'Doug has only scratched the surface to look at what *he* wants to concentrate on. He doesn't know what to do with the rest. It's only me that understands, for example, the sheer size of the information treasure chest

I've found at the law firm of Lemon, Lockhart & White. It's so much greater than Doug appreciates. He's not aware that I'm also working at the offices of Clifford & Gotch, Copthorne & Brookes's main rivals on the island – another source of fascinating files by the way. And I've kept shtum about working for the international division of JP Margeson, because he's had a mole in there and that's a bit too close to a conflict of interest even for me.'

'Wow. Why haven't you told him all this?'

'Need to know basis, Carey, need to know. You of all people must understand what I mean. Anyway, Doug is so obsessed with Copthorne & Brookes, and especially with Mike Peters and Wallace Copthorne, that I don't think he'd notice if I told him in great detail about everything else I'm uncovering. They're all he seems interested in at the moment, so I'm keeping the focus on them when I'm with him.'

'And he doesn't need to know? I thought you and he were working closely together.'

'We are ... working *very* closely, and that's been rather exciting, but let's just say I don't put all my eggs in one basket, Carey. Doug is cute and clever and it's fun to work into the night putting together a dossier, but there may be others I'm interested in getting to know ...'

Merino was processing the fact that he'd been told by Doug that Beatrice Goode was Dorian Miller's girl-friend, but this chick seemed to be saying that she and Doug would get it on from time to time. This was getting complicated – maybe some kind of Bermuda effect on people where cheating becomes a way of life and isn't confined to business.

Bee smiled, but her pout had the opposite effect to that intended and Merino brought the lunch to what she considered was a premature end. Blast! She'd even have to go back to *The Bugle's* offices and see Doug. Or maybe she could visit Dorian. Spoilt for choice.

'Do you mind if we go Dutch on lunch?' Merino asked.

This surprised Bee. What was that about? Keeping it formal? 'Gosh. You know how to treat a girl, don't you?'

'Sorry! Expenses, traceability and all that. Anyhow, I've a flight back to the US to catch, which I'm actually looking forward to for a change as I've got plenty to read. Doug gave me various bits of paperwork, which look very interesting indeed.'

'He didn't tell me what he'd given you. What was it?'

'You'd better check with him. Too much for me to list for you here and now, but there's a lot on Peters and Copthorne and stuff on the Bermuda Bond. If you've any additional paperwork on the Bond and CaBRe from the Lemon, Lockhart & White or JP Margeson files, perhaps you could drop it off at the American Consulate on Crown Hill. I've left instructions with them that anything marked for me is to be forwarded.'

'What about all the other material I've mentioned. That's worth something, isn't it?'

'I'll have a word back at the ranch.'

'Great. I'm sure we'll meet again,' said Bee and, as they stood up, she walked round the table and leant in to be kissed – a gesture which Merino duly ignored.

Playing hard to get, eh? Good job I like a challenge, Bee thought.

And she hadn't even told him she'd been called in by Gavin Boatwright to advise on a new booking system at Oxford Beaches. Gavin, the silver fox. Maybe I should pop over to see him, she thought. A lot of extremely interesting files were on *his* computer hard drive. What on earth would the FBI make of them?

Maybe she should give New York a try, perhaps staying for a couple of years if it got too hot on Bermuda for any reason.

9.

WILKINS

Eddie Wilkins was very pleased with the reports he was getting out of Bermuda.

Cogence had been very supportive when he suggested taking on Beatrice Goode and the quality of her information recently almost seemed 'too Goode to Bee true' as he said to his American boss in one of his dispatches.

Eddie once had a fling with Bee when she was working for *The Sunday Times* and they'd had a few too many drunken evenings at The Groucho Club. When they'd first met she boasted about having access to investigative reporters and that appealed to him as he wanted to get to know them.

Bee went cold on him soon after that, but they'd kept in touch and when she told him she was off to Bermuda on secondment, he offered her a retainer and a lucrative payment-by-results deal. Because of his unfinished business with Mike Peters, Wilkins thought she could be a useful resource to have based on the island.

It was going to cost him, having her based out there, but Cogence could hardly believe its luck when he started feeding through what Bee was uncovering. Goose and golden eggs came to mind as Wilkins ran through everything provided by her to date.

Based on the Bermuda Papers being assembled by Bee, he was able to hand over significant details of the financial assets of some wealthy individuals and corrupt public officials.

Encouraged, they gave him a 'shopping list' of key people they wanted background information on and were astounded when he could oblige.

Naturally, he gave them the impression that it required some considerable effort on his part to obtain the information, as well as the helpful support of his Bermuda associate.

Offshore shell company transactions for named individuals or international companies could be provided, and mining, computer, sportswear, and pharmaceutical companies could be searched for and located in the database, according to Bee. Wow! A gift that keeps on giving was how Wilkins saw it.

The fees and expenses Bee was racking up were now at a high level, but Cogence was more than happy to continue paying when Wilkins stressed how crucial he felt his operation on Bermuda was. Luckily, they never questioned that he might not be the real mastermind.

The latest conversation with Cogence was a boost to Wilkins.

'The work of your Bermuda agent has given us the edge on our competitors, Eddie. We're able to charge the earth in fees for certain pieces of corporate intelligence. We're heading towards being the number one agency worldwide,' his boss told him in a late afternoon call from Washington DC. 'I'll bet the POTUS himself couldn't find out what we know, and he's got the CIA behind him. All we've got is you and the Bermuda girl, Eddie. How about that?'

Wilkins mentally added a nought or two to next month's retainer invoice, and wondered if he should actually visit his bank account in Switzerland sometime soon.

*   *   *

Tipped off by Bee that Ash was likely to put the FBI in touch with him, Wilkins wasn't happy. Cogence wasn't happy.

Ash had called Wilkins, and spoken of his original meeting with Merino in New York. When told his name had been passed to the FBI, Wilkins easily feigned surprise and indignation because he really did think it was a 'bloody nuisance'.

'This could jeopardise my own operation,' Wilkins said to Ash over the phone.

'I thought you and they might have areas of mutual interest, you know, like Mike Peters and Wallace Copthorne.'

'I appreciate that, Ash, but it's a big deal getting involved with them. My associates at Cogence aren't going to be happy.'

'Why is that, Eddie? I thought you wanted all the dirt you could find on Copthorne & Brookes and were looking for a way to expose them. The FBI seem interested in the same things you are, isn't that right?'

'Well, yes, and, er, no, I suppose you could say.'

'You made enquiries with JP Margeson, didn't you, during the last conference and you know a lot about all sorts of financial jiggery-pokery that Peters gets up to. That'll be right up the FBI's avenue, won't it?'

'I hear what you're saying, Ash, but having the FBI crawling around is a whole different ball game – makes it take a sudden quantum leap to a far more serious level and very different from me trying to expose a fraudulent individual and his dodgy deals.'

'Surely the police or the authorities would have to be involved at some point if what you believe is true, don't you think?'

'I guess so. I'll try and see it as a positive, Ash, I promise.'

*   *   *

Now the FBI was coming to his office.

Wilkins sold it to his small team as being recognised internationally as the go-to firm for financial information.

'When international law enforcement agencies come knocking, it's either to arrest you or pick your brains,' he light-heartedly announced to his colleagues in their morning meeting. 'And, rest assured, they won't be arresting me this afternoon.'

Perhaps it was not the right thing to say. Too much of a mixed message he thought later when he became more and more aware of the jittery atmosphere in the office and the whispers by the front desk.

They actually think I'm going to be arrested, he realised. Well, I've given them a scare and it'll keep them on their toes. They'll soon see I was joking.

It was a formal visit. Carey Merino was very careful to show his ID at the front desk. It wasn't a low-key, incognito swing by the office.

Wilkins went to reception to meet and greet and to put his visitor and staff – who had miraculously congregated

– at ease, all in one handshake.

'Mr Merino – great to have you pop in to see us. I'm Eddie Wilkins.'

'Thanks, Eddie – a real pleasure to meet you. Thanks for sparing us the time.'

'Come through to my office and we'll organise a coffee,' Wilkins said to both Merino and the receptionist.

*   *   *

It turned out that Merino knew rather a lot of what Bee had reported to Wilkins. Strange.

'What's the source of your intelligence on the Bermuda Bond and Mike Peters in particular, Carey?' Wilkins asked.

'Wouldn't like to say, but a local journalist and someone he's close to, who seems to have some kind of inside access to local firms, have pieced together a useful dossier of allegations and leaked materials on subjects of interest to us. It helped flesh out our own enquiries in the US. And, I gather, there's more where that came from.'

Bee! And that Doug Bonsall, I bet, Wilkins guessed with no real mental exertion. What is she playing at?

'Mr Wilkins, I understand you have issues with Mike

Peters and evidence of historic fraud here in the UK. Is that so?'

That must have come from Ash, so it seems everyone is talking to the FBI. Wilkins tried to think how to play it. Informant, no, he didn't see himself as one of those. Investigator, yes, using knowledge as power, certainly, and never giving it away for nothing.

'Yes, I've been tracking him for a while. He did a moonlight flit from London and avoided court action.'

'What sort of case did you have against him?'

'All the papers are with a firm called Findlaters and I guess you'd need to get official sanction from them to take a look. I can tell you that, basically, Peters was helping himself, and that wife of his, to client funds and investing the money offshore. We suspected the Channel Islands or Bermuda and when he turned up eventually on Bermuda, well, that seemed to prove something.'

'So you let him get away with it?'

'I'd left Findlaters by then. They wouldn't play ball with me about access to the papers and, as the various clients had moved on, died, or lost interest, forensic accountants I consulted gave us zero chance of finding where the money had ended up, so –'

'You gave up?'

'No. I've been looking into Mike Peters again. I tried to warn Owen Ash and his Ashbury Events business about him because of the big conference organised with Copthorne & Brookes every couple of years on Bermuda.

I went to the last one and plan to go again this year, partly to keep an eye on what Peters is up to.'

'Why? What have you found?'

'I do some captive reinsurance for a few clients and Bermuda is the main place for that as far as the Brits are concerned. Peters and the senior guy at Copthorne & Brookes have their own captive, called CaBRe, and, between that enterprise and an investment fund called the Bermuda Bond which they've started, there are numerous transactions that would be worth you looking at.'

'Any UK parties involved?'

'According to my sources, yes, we've found quite a few who seem to have been compromised. We're getting in touch with them to see if we can help.'

'Are you going to involve the UK police?'

'Er, yes, if it gets to that point.'

'I don't think you should go rogue on these matters. You work with Cogence Inc out of Washington DC. Is that right, Mr Wilkins?'

How did they know that? Ash, most likely. Bee, perhaps?

'I'm only a humble associate. I hardly call the shots.'

'So they're after Peters too?'

'They've some very wealthy clients down in Florida who keep being fobbed off by the Bond company and they can't seem to get their money back. The returns are great, but the alarm bells are sounding. Cogence is interested in everything that Peters is involved in. I'm trying to help them by using my connections. Believe it or not, Peters himself was friendly to me when I last saw him and even told me an indiscreet story of how he'd helped a British arms dealer lodge his bribes from Saudi arms deals in accounts at the Bermudian bank, JP Margeson, and then magically made them disappear. I went to the bank but got given the cold shoulder. We've got an active investigation into Peters taking place on Bermuda at the moment.'

'Do you know an IT consultant currently on Bermuda called Beatrice Goode, Mr Wilkins?'

Why does he keep calling me Mr Wilkins when he asks a question? Do I assume he already knows the answer and is checking me out? Or is he bluffing?

'Ms Goode? Yes. I do, as a matter of fact. She does some freelance work for Cogence through me.'

Interesting, thought Merino. When I asked her who she worked for, she didn't mention Cogence or Wilkins, *and* she was offering to sell me stuff. Deciding not to sow the seed of discord between Wilkins and Beatrice Goode, at least not yet, Merino kept his response low key, but he put a little spanner in the works.

'I've seen her. She didn't mention you. Never mind. I assume then that you know she's involved with Doug Bonsall, a reporter on the island with *The Bugle*. I've seen him too, by the way.'

No wriggle room. And Bee, *involved* with Bonsall?

That was news. What the hell is going on out there?

'It seems you're much better informed than I am.' Wilkins hated admitting that. It hurt.

'Maybe. But that's why we should work together on this. I'll clear it with Cogence and presumably I can get your reports and other background details from them when I'm back in the US. You've been reasonably straight with me, so here's what we're going to do. I'm seeing Owen Ash and, with his cooperation, we're going to set up a sting at his next Bermuda Biennial and we're all going to work together to nail as many fraudsters as we can. How does that sound?'

'If Cogence is happy, then so am I. Is it going to be that easy though?'

'Who knows. But can we count on you and Beatrice to be part of the team?'

'I guess so, with the proviso I actually get the OK from Cogence.'

'I'll speak to Ash and we can all keep in touch and coordinate plans and pool information.'

Wilkins put on a cheerful face as he saw Merino off the premises – mainly for show – but inside he was seething. Talk about being outmanoeuvred. Did that matter? He wasn't sure.

At least the staff could see he wasn't being arrested.

10.

DORIAN

Dorian saw less of Bee. He knew she was working with Doug on some hush-hush project that was a vast undertaking for both of them and that she had also picked up a lot of extra clients.

As soon as she spoke to him about firewalls and protocols he switched off, and when she went on about complicated financial arrangements that were designed to avoid tax, disguise the source of funds and cloak everything in secrecy, he longed to get back to reading about events in the nineteenth century.

He tried to interest her more in the leisure activities that they enjoyed when they first met. Scuba and snorkelling off different parts of the island, with stopovers at the Swizzle Inn over on Blue Hole Hill. A Rum Swizzle, of course, and a fish sandwich after a morning swim with his girlfriend was Dorian's idea of heaven.

Lately, he'd lost count of the number of evenings he'd sat at Rosa's Cantina, nursing a Dos Equis beer and wondering if Bee would show.

'I'm working with Doug, but if we get through by nine, I'll come and join you,' was her response these days to an invite to dinner.

Maybe she isn't as keen on eating Rosa's chicken fajitas and iguana eggs as I am, Dorian thought. He was addicted to those stuffed jalapenos. Maybe the place isn't to her taste.

From time to time Dorian was in touch with Ash in the UK to keep him up to date and provide material for the next conference. He didn't report on his faltering relationship with Bee.

Although he threw himself into work and even took on some heritage tour-guide work outside of the Royal Naval Dockyard, Dorian spent more time on his own and a lot with Gavin Boatwright. That must have been why Gavin's ex-wife invited him to talk about his favourite books to her weekly book club at the Hamilton Princess. On Bermuda, everyone knew everyone else's business and their circles of friends overlapped almost completely.

*   *   *

'We had that rather dishy journalist come and interview us from *The Bugle*,' said Linda LaFong when Dorian sat down and poured himself some tea. 'You know him, don't you? When I rang to ask for his suggestions for possible speakers for our little book club, he recommended we get in touch with you. So glad you accepted, and, of course, we're all happy to make a donation to the Dockyard.'

'Yes, I know Doug Bonsall very well. He, like you, Linda, is a Bermudian born and bred and has been very good to me since I arrived. I saw the piece he wrote in the paper and thought you all sounded like an interesting bunch.'

Dorian had never thought of Doug as 'dishy', but what did he know of what constituted sex appeal?

'He's a good friend of mine, and a clever journalist who could go far.'

'He should be on TV. The local channel needs someone like him. I'll put in a word,' said Linda. 'Now, Dorian, what are you going to discuss with us today?'

'I thought we'd talk about the genius of CS Forester, perhaps a novelist you'd all dismiss as writing books for men.'

Various mumbles went round the table before Linda asked, 'Tell me, Dorian, do you only read novels with a naval flavour?'

'I suppose it is a special interest of mine, but Forester is more than that. He's famous for his naval books, of course, but I thought I'd talk about his crime novels

Payment Deferred, published in 1926, and *Plain Murder*, published in 1930, before moving on to talk about his novel *The African Queen*, which was made into a brilliant film in 1951 by John Huston. Plenty for us to get our teeth into and we'll gloss over the fact that the *African Queen* was actually a boat!'

Judging by the initial reaction to his chosen author, Dorian sensed his talk might be a bit of a challenge.

*   *   *

He needn't have worried as the session was a great success and Dorian surprised not only himself, but also the group who all promised to read some CS Forester.

Linda invited him down to the hotel bar for a drink to 'thank him properly' but he guessed what was coming.

'How well do you know Gavin, my ex?' she asked.

'It's a bit awkward, I know, but actually I'm not one to take sides in a split, so I'll steer clear of that, if you don't mind.'

'Not a bit, Dorian, I'm happily married now to Mr LaFong, and, as he spends most of his time in Hong Kong and Singapore, I've discovered what may be the secret of a good relationship.'

'I'm pleased for you.'

'But you and your friend Doug should both be wary of Gavin, you know. He's charm on legs, but his past wouldn't bear scrutiny and he's more of a CS Forester crime baddie than a Hornblower.'

'This is difficult, Linda, as Gavin's a great friend and benefactor who has been hugely generous with his time and money as far as the Dockyard and me, personally, are concerned. I'm even staying, at his expense, at Oxford Beaches.'

'As a friend he's perfect. All I'm saying is that as a business or marriage partner, he's not to be trusted.'

*　　　*　　　*

It unnerved Dorian and even though he dismissed it as typical of the snide remarks made by divorced couples, it had coloured his thinking about Gavin.

He passed on his concerns to Doug who, at first, was equally sceptical, but when they both reviewed what they knew about Gavin, even about his relationship with Fiona Peters, they had to agree that maybe there was something in it.

That led to Dorian trying to engage Gavin in

conversation late one night about how he'd done as well as he had in the business world.

'Lucky breaks, my boy, in the main. Who can say what makes one man get those breaks. Being in the right place at the right time, seizing every opportunity, making your own success, sticking to your guns, striking out on your own ... Who knows? All those clichés are true.'

'What one thing has made you so successful financially?'

'Dorian, why are you suddenly so interested in money? To use yet another cliché, money isn't everything, you know. In fact, one of the things I like about you is that you're happy to work at what you love and, presumably, you're not in it for the money.'

'That's true, yes, but because your life is such a contrast with what I know, I find it fascinating.'

'A word to the wise, Dorian, making money, and a lot of it, can be a nasty business. The sort of world I was in, the so-called leisure industry, was not enjoyable at all when I look back on it. It was full of rogues and chancers as well as borderline and full-blown criminals and gangsters. I don't really like or want to talk about it, if you don't mind. Let's get back to you telling me which is your favourite nautical film.'

That was as far as Dorian's investigations took him and the subject was never again raised with Gavin, who didn't seem to have taken offence.

On one occasion Gavin entertained Dorian and Bee

to dinner at Dennis's Hideaway, a half-mythical, totally eccentric restaurant over towards St David's.

This was Gavin's favourite eatery on Bermuda and he was a friend of the owner, the piratical looking Dennis Lamb. They all ate 'fish dinner with the works': a feast of shark hash on toast, conch fritters, fish chowder, shrimp, scallops, and fried fish – as well as a bit of mussel pie.

Dorian felt that he, Gavin and Bee bonded over that dinner and he wasn't surprised that on hearing about Bee's computer wizardry, Gavin asked her to pop over to take a look at the IT system that so frustrated him at Oxford Beaches.

'Dinner's definitely on me – great company, and a new consultant signed up,' Gavin said, as he waved a large stash of notes at Dennis in payment of the bill.

Dorian enjoyed the fact that Bee got on so well with his friends. That was a good thing in his view and a stark contrast to his exes who'd often complained that the people he knew were boring. And his friends seemed to like her.

It was a good sign for their relationship, wasn't it?

11.

Ash

Ash was sitting in the book-lined room of Anthony de Rivaulx QC, who usually charged over a thousand pounds an hour for a consultation. His chambers were in Gray's Inn and handy for Ash to call in at drinks time and share a glass of Islay malt on his way home.

They often met and more so recently to discuss topics that de Rivaulx could speak on for Ashbury Events. He was worth every penny of the huge fee he charged, because he could be guaranteed to sell out any tax conference he spoke at.

Top secrecy jurisdictions, tax optimisation, asset protection, efficient corporate structures – all designed to hide things and complicate matters so little or no tax would be paid. That's what de Rivaulx specialised in.

Vendors of tax schemes would go to him for an opinion

on whether or not this or that plan would actually work. One example he used in his talks was of a multinational company with a head office in the US who located its company brand in Ireland, its shipping arm on the Isle of Man, its management expertise in Switzerland and its reinsurance subsidiary on Bermuda. With sleight of hand and a few visuals, de Rivaulx would show the paper trail and demonstrate where the final profits were made. He would defy anyone to disprove how much any of the other centres contributed to profits and costs. 'Nobody can say for sure,' he would announce, 'so the accountants can make it all up.' A tour de force of transfer pricing and legal tax avoidance exposition. Conference box office gold.

His personal position on tax was, in contrast, rather simple and straightforward, as he believed it was always better to pay the tax due. He often said, 'You can't avoid all taxes – for example, waiting is a tax on travel, stress a tax on success, heartache a tax on love, and illness a tax on life.'

To Ash, Anthony de Rivaulx QC was an old friend who didn't seem to mind having his brain picked from time to time, unlike most barristers who would charge for being asked the time of day.

With an enviable reputation for being the only person in Chancery clever enough to understand the more complicated tax avoidance schemes and the most complex commercial fraud cases, where better for Ash to discuss his involvement with the FBI?

'I've somehow got myself engaged in an ongoing FBI investigation on some international financial fraud and I don't know what the legal implications are for me and how best I should play it.'

'If you're seriously engaged with them, Ash, you'd better speak to someone at the Serious Fraud Office. I can recommend one of their chief investigators – the brightest one that I've come across. She knows the form for this type of case and could point you in the right direction at least. She might even want to speak to the FBI herself if what they've found is of relevance to UK resident companies or individuals.'

'The problem is, I don't want to set any hares running. I was hoping to operate without getting in too deep – just assist the FBI, facilitate what they want to do, and then let them get on with it.'

'You don't want to spend any money getting proper legal advice more like, you cheapskate.'

'I'm due to see the FBI chap. He's flying in to London sometime. I thought you might be able to at least put my mind at rest.'

'Have you done anything illegal?'

'No.'

'Is he going to be seeing the UK authorities?'

'I don't know.'

'That would be normal for an international operation like this. I suggest you wait and see. Ask him who he's involving over here. Anyway, whilst you're drinking my best malt, you'd better tell me what's going on. Establish the facts, Ash. That's always my starting point.'

'As far as I can make out, there's a firm on Bermuda where a couple of the partners have what the FBI think is a Ponzi scheme that is somehow linked to a captive insurance company they've set up.'

'Hang on a minute. If this is Bermuda, is the FBI guy working with the local police on any of this?'

'Not yet, I don't think.'

'Sorry, you were saying? Carry on.'

'I know a couple of people who work for the local paper out there – Doug Bonsall and Beatrice Goode – who are running their own investigation, working together on a dossier of papers they've acquired from a Bermudian bank and other professional firms.'

'Stop there. Are these freelance investigators in touch with the FBI or the local police?'

'Yes.'

'This sounds like Scooby-Doo does fraud busting. Ash, it's far more serious than you think. You know a bit too much to pretend to be an innocent bystander. If I were you, I'd get in touch with my Serious Fraud Office contact as she may know a tame officer at Scotland Yard you can talk to.'

'I'll do that after I've seen the FBI bloke.'

'I'm more intrigued by the papers you mentioned just now and what your Velma and Shaggy are up to. That sounds to me like they're engaged in criminal activity if they're actually stealing confidential files.'

'Oh, the FBI knows all about that, I think. Don't worry. It doesn't involve yours truly.'

*   *   *

Ash met Carey Merino at the offices of Ashbury Events in Victoria.

'Welcome to London – are you seeing anyone else on this trip?' Ash greeted him.

'Yes. I've seen a guy at Scotland Yard, who's also put me in touch with a senior officer on Bermuda. I've quite a network in place since we last spoke: a fraud expert with the Royal Canadian Mounted Police, a high-level officer with the Bermuda Police and a real tough inspector at Scotland Yard. Funnily enough, they've worked together before, so that's all good.'

'Ah. Do they know about me?'

'Yes. They know you're key to this operation working when we get to Bermuda.'

'Key? As in involved? I hope that doesn't link me too closely with all this?'

'Relax. They know you're helping me, that's all. Your contacts on Bermuda are crucial and so is Eddie Wilkins, thanks to your tip.'

'Wilkins?'

'Seen him too.'

'You have been busy.'

'And, I nearly forgot, the stuff that those two private investigators have produced has been instrumental in getting FinCEN very excited.'

'FinCEN?'

'Sorry, that's the US Treasury's Financial Crimes Enforcement Agency. Not long set up and recently merged with the Treasury Department's Office of Financial Enforcement. That means we've got some big guns on this and we're getting really organised.'

'Did Wilkins prove helpful?'

'Yes, he did. Strange character. Works for a corporate intelligence company and has his own agent on Bermuda.'

'Who's that, if you can tell me?'

'Beatrice Goode – I thought you would have known.'

'I'd no idea she worked with Wilkins. I doubt her boyfriend does either, or Doug. Do you know if they do?'

'Blowed if I know. Seems to me that she and Doug are pretty close. Maybe he knows. I don't know her other boyfriend.'

'Dorian Miller.'

'Doug mentioned him, but she seems – how shall I put it – to be capable of playing away from home, if you get my drift.'

'Really? I'm out of touch here in London. Maybe you

should leave me out of all this.'

'No chance. Like I've said, you're key. That's what I want to talk about. We need to bug some of the rooms at the conference. To film and record the private break-out sessions.'

'Come on. I can't allow that. What about the responsibilities I have to respect the privacy of my delegates? Doesn't that infringe some kind of amendment in your country?'

Strange, Ash, thought, how much more confident he felt talking to the FBI here in London. Merino didn't seem to mind.

'We're way past that. The hotel knows what we're doing. Blame them. The Bermuda Police know what we're doing. Blame them. We'll have all the warrants in place that we need. Now, tell me, who's your technical guy? We're going to need to work with him. A couple of my guys, real covert snoopers, will be alongside him. They can also handle all the audio-visual stuff at the event. Nobody'll suspect a thing. Can you trust your guy to play ball? Who is he? Can I meet him?'

'He's ... Ben. Er, Ben Sanchez. He's very well known to us, good at what he does, a sound guy, sorry, I mean that we trust him. He's not one of our employees, but we use him a lot. He's coming to the event to handle the techie side of things for us as part of our team.'

'Who else are you taking?'

'Just a couple of others from our own staff.'

'Can you set up a meeting, say for tomorrow afternoon, so I can come in and brief them?'

'Actually, no, I'm not going to do that. I've taken some top legal advice of my own and I've already decided what to do as far as the conference is concerned.'

'You're not gonna bail out on us?'

'No. Not at all, I think it best if I, er, we at Ashbury Events concentrate on running the event as normal so as not to arouse any suspicions. To us, you'll just be treated like any other delegate. We'll be there at The Hamilton Princess running our Bermuda Biennial as we usually do. That way we can't compromise anything by saying or doing the wrong thing and will leave you to get on with your business.'

'Fine. I can live with that, but what about this Ben Sanchez? What are we going to do about him?'

'I'll call him and put him in the picture. He's an interesting bloke and has done all sorts of things, including – he once told me – doing some work for MI5, so you and he will probably talk the same language. Where are you staying? I'll tell him to call you as soon as possible.'

'I'm at St Ermin's Hotel, Westminster. You can leave a message under my name. I'm sure we'll be able to work with this Sanchez. I'll have a couple of our guys assisting him, but if he won't play ball at any stage, we'll replace him completely and he can go and sit by the pool.'

'I hope that won't be necessary.'

'No, but all I'm saying is that running a few visuals

and the sound system for a conference like yours would be a walk in the park for us. We won't mess it up, don't worry. By the way, can you let me have a list of people attending the event? I'll need it updated every week until we get there. And, one more thing, who's the dame called Harriet Hall? She used to work for you, I believe.'

'Harriet Hall?'

'Yes, Harriet Hall. It turns out she's on Bermuda, working with Peters.'

'Really? She used to work on the event for us. She and Copthorne & Brookes are as thick as thieves, if you'll pardon the expression. She's supposed to have had an affair with one of the partners and they were mightily miffed when we parted company with her. What's she doing out there?'

'Get this. She's running some kind of brothel, apparently, if you can believe your friend Doug. He thinks that's partly how they entice punters into their net so that they end up investing with them to avoid being blackmailed. Or is that blackmail anyway? I don't know. Thought you'd be interested. I take it *you* don't run that kind of service for delegates?'

*   *   *

Ash felt badly informed. Doug had not kept him, or presumably Dorian up to speed, because if he had, then surely Dorian would have told him.

This had all set him thinking …

Wilkins, what a dark horse. Corporate intelligence are two words that don't often go together and certainly not when applied to him. But he's outwitted us and has Bee as a spy in our camp. She's kept her work with Wilkins and Cogence a secret. What a piece of work. Poor Dorian.

Still, at least Merino has made everything official and clarified my role in all this. I'm a facilitator, that's all. The middle man, the means, not the end. That's a relief. That puts me and Ashbury Events in the clear, doesn't it? Observers, not participators – spectators, not players.

And Merino's insinuations about Bee and Doug – that makes things very messy. Does Doug know about Bee's connection with Wilkins? That could change things between them. Where does it put Bee and Dorian? Or Dorian and Doug? Is this some weird variation on the Bermuda Triangle mystery, only this time a *ménage-à-trois* where loyalty goes out of the window, friendship gets sucked into some kind of paranormal vortex and trust disappears?

So much for our Elbow Beach declaration and bonding experience.

PART THREE

BERMUDA, AUTUMN 1995

12.

SATURDAY

Ash landed at Bermuda airport on the afternoon flight from Gatwick and knew there was a good hour or so of sunlight remaining.

With Dawn Grainger and Ben Sanchez travelling with him, it meant that the key members of the team running that week's big conference for Ashbury Events had arrived.

They were happy with all their preparations over the previous days and months. Dawn was relying on a couple of local agency staff to assist on each day with the admin elements of the event, and Ben was to meet his new two-man, audio-visual support crew in a day or so.

Working with the FBI was a prospect Ben took in his stride and Carey Merino had been impressed with him when they'd met in London a few months back

– especially with his experience of working undercover on National Crime Agency and MI5 operations.

Dawn was, however, slightly apprehensive that the operations side of the conference was going to function smoothly, given the FBI's sideshow.

'Your job is just to concentrate on running the event as you normally would. Don't think about anything else,' was how Ash put it in the taxi over to the Hamilton Princess when Dawn questioned the whole set-up again.

'And you, Ben, you're here to make sure the technical side works without a hitch, no matter what nefarious activities you're getting up to with your other boss,' Ash added.

'And what will *you* be doing, Ash?' asked Dawn.

'Me? Oh, I'll be trying, and failing, to keep Copthorne & Brookes happy, same as usual.'

'Won't you be enjoying the clandestine goings on?' Ben said.

'Not if I can help it. I'll be able to turn a blind eye to it all with any luck.'

*   *   *

They unpacked and met as arranged in the Colony Pub for a Dark 'n' Stormy.

A flier on the table posed the question 'Can you take the heat?' with details of that evening's entertainment in the Gazebo Lounge of the hotel.

Insisting that the only way to fight jet lag was to prolong the evening beyond the point of your body telling you to flake out, Ash persuaded Dawn and Ben to accompany him to Tropical Heatwave – an all-island revue starring Gene Steede and the Bermuda Triangle Band.

'What, they'll actually be playing triangles?' said Ben, deadpan, reading the leaflet.

'Uh, no,' replied Ash. 'Very amusing. Look, it'll be fun. He's the island's superstar and a great entertainer. He's even funnier than you are, Ben. It'll be great, infectious calypso music. Everyone who sees him likes him and enjoys the show. And, we won't need to eat as we're still stuffed from the plane. Look, the cover charge of thirty-five Bermudian dollars includes two drinks *and* the show. It says here it's a "Jump Up and Dance" evening – what better way to guarantee we don't fall asleep until later. We'll all feel better for it in the morning.'

They were soon singing along to Gene Steede's version of the Caribbean classic song, 'Feeling Hot Hot Hot':

Ole ole, ole ole, ole ole, ole ole, Me mind on fire – Me soul on fire – Feeling hot hot hot, Party people – All around me feeling hot hot hot.

They were enjoying a fun evening and it seemed natural for them to volunteer to join in with the limbo dancing at the end when Gene Steede called for audience participation. After a couple of lowerings of the flaming bar and a few more rousing choruses of 'Hot Hot Hot', Ash was surprised when Mike Peters and his wife Fiona appeared beside him.

'Great to see you back on Bermuda, Ash. Come on! Show us what you can do,' said Mike Peters. 'Arch that back, get down on it, and limbo through.'

It was Ash's turn, so he didn't have the chance to reply as the other participants were urging him to get a move on. He tried to bend and wriggle his body under the limbo bar.

It was perhaps inevitable that Mike Peters would help him. He was that kind of guy. A casual nudge with his foot on Ash's shoulder and another limbo novice was eliminated.

Flat on his back, Ash managed a 'How low can you go?' to Peters as he saw him and his wife smilingly wave goodbye and leave the stage.

'Actually the show was a great start to our week here, Ash, you were right,' Dawn said, as they picked up their keys at reception. 'But that guy Peters. Isn't he a jerk?'

'Forget about him. He didn't really spoil the fun,' Ash managed to reply without showing how pissed off with Peters he really was.

'What's the plan for tomorrow?' asked Ben.

'Well, as we can't do any setting up until Monday, I suggest we all have a free day. Go to the pool or the beach, or hit the shops. Your choice. I might catch up with Dorian. I said I would, so I feel obligated,' Ash replied.

'I'm going snorkelling, Dawn. Care to join me?' offered Ben.

'I'll probably check all the event boxes are here and then have a lazy day in the hotel,' she said.

'OK, let's all have dinner over at the Seahorse Grill at Elbow Beach tomorrow night. I'll fix it,' said Ash as they said their goodnights and headed off to their rooms.

13.

SUNDAY

The following morning, the single sheet of Roneod paper slipped under each guest room door forecast a sunny day, with highs of twenty-eight degrees. Ash picked it up and wished he didn't have to meet up with Dorian, fond of him though he was. He could do with a day by the pool but he reminded himself that it was a working week and not likely to be a fun one – Peters's little prank the night before demonstrated that.

Reading on through the forecast, Ash noticed it gave a warning of a possible hurricane for the end of the week. How fitting was that? It matched the way he viewed the likely outcome for the week in prospect more accurately than the sunshine outside apparently prophesied.

Ash went down to breakfast in the hotel's Tiara Room and was surprised to see Dawn and Ben already there.

They were sitting together at a table by the window that had a great view of the harbour, which took your eye away from the excess of mauve in the decor of the restaurant.

'We liaised,' explained Dawn.

'I see you're not eating a Bermuda Sunday breakfast of codfish and potatoes,' Ash said, eyeing their plates of bacon, eggs and pancakes.

'We'll leave that for you, Ash,' said Ben. 'We thought we'd have an early start as we're taking the hotel boat over to the other side of the harbour. We want to get ourselves to the beach at the Southampton Princess – I've read it's great for snorkelling and Dawn is going to give it a try, aren't you, Dawn?'

'Sure am. And probably have a few frozen pina coladas at the beach bar.'

'Oh. I see. What happened to the "I'll check all the event boxes" ...'

'You know, I realised you were right yesterday about taking the day off. Ben talked me into going snorkelling. How about you? What are you going to do?'

'Actually, that little thing last night with Peters bugged me – no pun intended, Ben, that's really your department. It's put me into work mode, so I'll see Dorian and maybe even catch up with Doug Bonsall, the journalist I've told you about. You two have fun and meet me here at seven tonight. We'll take it from there.'

Dawn and Ben seemed in a hurry to Ash, because they quickly finished their breakfasts and left. Ash went over to get a plate of fruit and picked up a copy of *The Bugle*, glancing through it with a cup of coffee.

What caught his eye was a 'Latest News' piece, headed 'Missing Banker's Body Found':

The body of the banker William Cloudesley, 41, has been found, several weeks after he was reported missing. The body was found in the underground water cistern at his home and the death is being treated as suspicious.

Ash knew straight away that this was Doug's mole at JP Margeson. When told a while ago that the guy had gone missing, Ash just thought he must have done a bunk, fleeing the bank, leaving his wife and getting off the island. But he knew Doug didn't see it that way.

Dorian had first reported the disappearance to Ash a month or two back when he rang to say, 'Doug's bank informant has gone off radar. Doug thinks he's been bumped off and says someone must have found out he was acting as a mole.'

Subsequently, Dorian rang again: 'Doug has seen the bank mole's wife. The plot thickens. Turns out the guy's passport, wallet and all of his belongings are still at the house. He's officially a missing person, but the police are concerned for his welfare. But get this, the wife and the police can't find his phone or his computer. Now Doug is even more convinced than ever the guy's been bumped off. It's making him twitchier and twitchier about his own safety and security. He thinks that once the authorities find out what was on the bloody computer and that he was making frequent phone calls to Doug, it could spell real trouble and drag Doug into it. That's why he's in a real state and the trouble is, I think he got Bee involved with the mole as well.'

'Doug should tell the police and maybe, if he can't get anywhere with the local force, you should tell him to inform Carey Merino.'

'He's frightened to go to the police as they already have him marked down as a crank and he doesn't want to get himself implicated. I'm more worried about Bee. She won't tell me whether or not she was involved with this guy. All she says is that her consultancy work was with the bank and she had no more contact with the mole than she did with any other employee.'

That was how it had been left.

Ash re-read the snippet in the paper. The mole ends up underground – how fitting, Ash thought.

Suicide might be an explanation. Maybe a mole with cold feet?

What grounds were there for thinking the death suspicious? It usually meant that suicide had already been ruled out. Looks like Doug was right after all.

It was the start to the week that Ash had dreaded.

*   *   *

Ash rang Dorian, half expecting him to be with Bee, but found him on his own and at a loose end.

'I was hoping you'd call, Ash. I assumed you'd be in on the Saturday BA flight.'

'Yes, we got in last night. I wondered if you'd be around for a spot of lunch, around one-ish at Harley's Bistro here at the hotel?'

'Sure, see you then. It'll just be me, Bee's working flat out on some project or other.'

After a stroll along Front Street, Ash was back at the hotel, sipping a beer at Harley's and speculating on what was going on between Bee and Dorian. He was ready for lunch and knew Dorian was amused by the mild nautical theme of the poolside restaurant overlooking the harbour.

When Dorian arrived, they both ordered the curried shrimp and scallops en brochette. As soon as Dorian had a beer in front of him, Ash asked him a direct question.

'Before we talk about the conference and everything else, Dorian, you'd better tell me how things are going with Bee.'

'Mixed, I'd have to say. We rarely see each other these days. Pressure of work, she says, but I'm not so sure. I know that she does have a shedload of work as she's got so many clients. Once word got round she was a Y2K expert, seems everyone on the island with a computer system wanted her to take a look.'

'That's clever marketing on her part, Dorian. You have

to hand it to her.'

'I do. Everyone in financial services is shit-scared of Millenium bug problems, but she thinks it's all a con.'

'But she's laughing all the way to the bank, right?'

'Yes, she's cashing in on the panic. She says, quite openly to me at least, that people plus computers equals gullibility. Y2K gives her access to all areas apparently. It's led to her being called in by JP Margeson and loads of other companies, as well as by Gavin for the hotel computer system.'

'JP Margeson? Isn't that where William Cloudesley worked, whose body has just been found?'

'Yes, that's it. He was Doug's mole originally, but now both Bee and Doug are twitchy about being traced. They got mountains of material from him.'

'They'll have to go to the police, won't they?'

'They won't, unless the police go to them. They might speak to the FBI guy about it or might have already done so, but to be honest, Ash, I wouldn't know. I'm out of the loop. Doug and Bee spend an awful lot of time together these days and I don't know what stage they're at with their own investigations.'

Ash felt terrible about not voicing the suspicions about Doug and Bee that he heard from Carey Merino when they'd met in London.

'But you're still in a relationship with Bee, aren't you?'

'Sort of, but we meet up maybe once or twice a week at most. She sometimes comes over to Oxford Beaches when I'm at the Dockyard, and spends all the time closeted with Gavin, apparently. They have lunch together, according to the maitre d', who seems to think I should be told. When I get back she's gone, leaving me a note to apologise that she's way behind on some project and can't hang around to see me.'

'That doesn't sound good to me, Dorian.'

'Dead right it doesn't, but things have been very strange the past month or so.'

'How so?'

'Where do I start? First of all, like I said, Doug has been getting very anxious. I speak to him on the phone and he seems preoccupied all the time and can rarely make time to meet up, even for a drink. I mean how busy can a journalist on the local rag be? When I do speak to him, he goes off on a number – usually about Peters, but now this missing banker has sent him into a tailspin.'

'What's been happening?'

'He's getting paranoid. He's convinced he's being followed, for a start. You heard about his mugging, didn't you? Well, he thinks it could happen again at any time.'

'I thought after the second alleged attack, things had gone quiet?'

'Not according to Doug, but that's Doug for you. Everything's a drama. Anyway, enough about him. The real story is Harriet Hall.'

'I heard she was on the island and up to no good.'

'That's putting it mildly. She's everywhere – every

social event. In the newspaper on the social pages, the business pages, writing interior design features, and even popping up on TV.'

'Any indication of what she's up to with Copthorne & Brookes?'

'What, apart from trying to book the Dockyard as well as the Southampton Princess for a reinsurance event, you mean?'

'How did you find that out?'

'It's a small island, Ash. The Dockyard's Commercial Director told me about La Hall's approach in connection with a Copthorne & Brookes cocktail evening to be held during a big reinsurance conference planned for next year. Everyone knows I speak for your event, so they asked me if I knew anything about it. What do you make of that? What a nerve, eh.'

'Inevitable, I suppose. Have you met Harriet?'

'Yes. She marched straight up to my table one evening at Rosa's Cantina and introduced herself. She was with Mike Peters and his wife who waved to me from the other side of the restaurant. I was on my own – Bee was held up again – so she plonked herself down and asked me if I was happy speaking for you, given you were not highly thought of on Bermuda.'

'Charming! That's the competitive world of conferences, Dorian, but look at who she's ended up with. People, like water, find their own level. Isn't that what they say?'

'She also rather cheekily asked me who I was waiting for. "Is it that very pretty girlfriend of yours," she said. I then, of course, had to ask her how she knew Bee. No doubt as she'd intended to do all along, she told me that Bee and Doug had been pointed out to her by Mike Peters when they were seen walking together along Front Street. Then she added, "And now I keep seeing them together everywhere."'

'What did you make of that?'

'It unsettled me, I can tell you, but I've tried hard not to let the green-eyed monster of jealousy get to me. I saw it affect my mother's life and don't want to jump to any wrong conclusions. I know that Doug sees an awful lot of Bee, but try to push that out of my head and trust them both, but I don't know what to think. Just to confuse things even more, Doug rang me up a little while ago and asked if I knew where she was. I said I thought she was with him, but he was checking to see if she was with me! It would seem that neither Doug nor I have seen much of Bee lately, if he's to be believed, but I honestly don't know. The last time I saw Bee, I raised the issue with her, but she just told me not to be so stupid and that she couldn't help having so much work on.'

Ash fought the urge to tell Dorian about Carey Merino's thoughts on Doug and Bee's relationship.

They then spoke about the upcoming conference, running through the partners' programme, before Dorian announced he'd have to head off to do some work on a new book he was writing on Bermuda and The Royal Navy.

*   *   *

'We've had a very interesting few weeks here on Bermuda,' Doug replied when Ash rang him later and asked him how life was going.

Before phoning, Ash had enjoyed an hour or two by the pool after his vaguely unsettling lunch with Dorian. That was why he'd decided to try and play relationship counsellor.

'Look, Doug, I'll be completely open with you. It was hinted to me that you and Bee were very close.'

'Who by? Dorian?'

'No, somebody else.'

'Well I don't know what you've been told, but in any case, I haven't seen much of her recently. She spends all her time with Gavin it seems. I rang Dorian once to ask if she was with him and he said he thought she was with me. If anything, she's two-timing both of us with someone new. Maybe Gavin.'

'If you think she's two-timing you, that suggests you and she were in some kind of relationship.'

'You seem to already know something, so I'll tell you – I've felt terrible about it. I'm not sure what Dorian knows.'

'Well, he certainly suspects something, Doug.'

'God, that makes me feel worse. Bee doesn't seem to care. Calls herself a free spirit and a born romantic who falls in love at the drop of a hat.'

'What makes you think there's anything going on with her and Gavin of all people?'

'He's mega-rich. He's got film-star looks. He owns a yacht and a hotel. Do I need to go on?'

'Put like that, I see your point, but I didn't see her as a gold-digger. She and Dorian seemed right for each other.'

'That's why I feel so bad about things. It just happened. She took the initiative, Ash, honest. She gave me a big frenchie one evening when we were working late and that was it.'

'What's happened with Gavin then to make you think she's turned her attention to him?'

'I've actually got friendly with Gavin's ex, Linda LaFong, who has asked me to ghost write her autobiography under the title *If Moolah be the Food of Love ... Pay On*. As you can tell from that, she has some interesting things to say about the source of Gavin's wealth. She's obsessed with him really and somehow keeps tabs on his movements even implying that Gavin and Bee spend nights together at Oxford Beaches or on his yacht.'

'Really? Dorian told me she was working with the hotel on its IT systems.'

'Nobody, not even Bee is that keen on IT, Ash. But, get this – in the early days of her looking at the computers at Oxford Beaches, Bee said she'd found files that record the sources of Gavin's wealth and movements of funds around the tax havens. I got interested and asked for more information, but the next time I saw her, she clammed up. Maybe that's when they'd crossed the line in their relationship.'

'What a bloody mess, Doug, and I thought you and Dorian were great friends.'

'I'll have to see Dorian and talk about it sometime, but I just can't face it. I feel bad enough about it now without confronting him, and I can't see how bringing it all out into the open would help.'

'Bee doesn't exactly come out of this well either, does she. Dorian needs to know that about her, and soon. I'll have a think about how we should play this. In the meantime, how worried are you about what seems to have happened to your bank mole? I saw the latest in the paper this morning.'

'William Cloudesley? For me, it's a disaster waiting to happen. I think it must have something to do with Peters. I've held off doing anything until I can maybe go to the police with Carey Merino. A bit of FBI backing might help me. The local force think I've cried wolf too many times as it is. I'm concerned about the position that I'm in because he was my source, but that affects Bee as well.'

'Do you know any more than was in *The Bugle*?'

'Yes. He was badly beaten before he died.'

'Oh my God, so why are you convinced Peters is behind it?'

'One of Cloudesley's colleagues told him that the audit partner from Copthorne & Brookes kept asking who exactly from the bank could access the CaBRe and Bermuda Bond accounts. He didn't know why the auditor kept harping on about it. Now we know, don't we.'

'Does Peters know there's been a leak of information then?'

'He must do. What other explanation is there?'

'Let's hope there is another one. Maybe Cloudesley was having an affair that went wrong.'

'We'll see. In the meantime, how's this year's event shaping up?'

'The event itself is fine. I'm worried about all the other stuff planned. Much as *you* seem to be, I'm awaiting the arrival of Carey Merino from New York tomorrow. Have you had much contact with him?'

'A bit. He got all my information some time ago and, apparently, doesn't want me poking around any more. I heard from Scott, my pal on the local police, that they're going to be involved with the FBI enquiry, but even *he* wouldn't tell me any more. What can *you* tell me? Anything?'

'Not a lot, Doug, no. I'm trying to concentrate on being a conference organiser. I'm facilitating access to the event for the FBI, but that's where I've drawn the line on my involvement.'

Doug and Ash agreed to speak soon with Doug confirming he'd be covering the conference for *The Bugle*.

Ash felt that things needed to be sorted out between Dorian and Doug, and even Bee, before the conference started. It now seemed that neither Doug nor Dorian knew of the connection between Bee and Wilkins, as surely one of them would have mentioned it if they did. How on earth would that play out? Ash felt sure that Gavin wouldn't be happy knowing about Bee's association with Wilkins either, particularly about them working in cahoots with a company like Cogence and now the FBI. Oh dear. Talk about storm clouds brewing.

*   *   *

The evening at the Seahorse Grill at Elbow Beach hotel was calming. Ash could tell that there was obviously something going on between Dawn and Ben, but, hey, they're young and single, he thought, so why not? Even if he did feel a bit of a gooseberry, it meant that the evening went by in jovial fashion.

Conversation was very light-hearted as they dined

on Dark 'n' Stormy chilled soups and Bermuda honey-glazed wahoo.

The evening was relaxed and happy, but because of their lingering jet lag, they were content to round it off with an Armagnac and get a taxi back to the Hamilton Princess.

Hearing about Dawn and Ben's day exploring the beach at Horseshoe Bay and snorkelling in the sheltered cove of the Southampton Princess, Ash was reminded why he liked Bermuda so much. He envied them their day, which seemed to have been perfect – apart from their sighting of a poisonous lionfish, which struck Ash as an omen and reminder of the threats that can lie just beneath the surface.

14.

It was eight-thirty. Ash was on the point of leaving his room to head to the executive lounge on the sixth floor for a continental breakfast and a quick look at *The Bugle* when his doorbell rang.

Thinking it might be room service, he opened the door casually to find Carey Merino standing there.

'Hello, Mr Ash, mind if I join you?'

Having no choice in the matter, Ash waved him in.

'Sorry to disturb you, but I wanted to catch you early. I got in yesterday, but ... well, it was the weekend, so I thought I'd leave you to enjoy it. Now, today, well, that's different. We need to set some ground rules for the week ahead.'

'They're predicting storms, maybe even a hurricane, Mr Merino. What are you forecasting?'

'A calm week – we've done most of our investigative work and that means the next few days should be quite relaxed in my opinion. It's a surveillance week. We'll work with Ben Sanchez to make sure we're all set up to record what happens in the break-out rooms. Naturally, with the cooperation of the hotel and the local police, we're doing a bit more than that, but nothing that concerns you.'

'What, so I just get on with running the event?'

'That's what you wanted, isn't it? You do your thing and leave everything else to us.'

'Yes, but what about Doug Bonsall, for example? He wants to see you, not least because there's the recent murder of his mole at JP Margeson to factor in. And what about Eddie Wilkins? Just where do Doug and Eddie come into all this?'

'And don't forget the dame.'

'Bee, Beatrice Goode?'

'Yes. She's been in constant touch with me of late trying to get us interested in files on various people on the island that have links to some high-level felons in the US. She's a real bloodhound that one. I wonder if Wilkins knows half of what she's up to. Still, that's not my problem. We're primarily after Mike Peters and this Bermuda Bond of his. After that, the next element of import for us is his reinsurance racket. Anything else local we'll leave to the Bermudians. And everything else we know about US-based fraudsters, we'll deal with back at home.'

'Has Beatrice told you anything about Gavin Boatwright?'

'You might say that.'

'And?'

'And, nothing, Mr Ash. I think it's better that you're kept in the dark. Just don't go into business with him, or even split a restaurant bill, that's all I'd say to you.'

✳   ✳   ✳

Ash, deciding to skip breakfast, headed off with Merino to the hotel conference suite.

He was relieved to see Dawn and Ben had beaten them to it and were finishing a conversation with a member of the banqueting team when he and Merino arrived to join them.

'Good timing, Ash, we're just arranging for all our gear to be brought up from the bowels of the hotel,' Dawn said.

'You both know Carey Merino,' Ash said. 'The guys who'll be helping on the techie side are waiting in the coffee shop. Why don't you head down there with Mr Merino, Ben, until all your kit has been brought up.'

Ash was pleased to have a moment alone with Dawn.

'So, any change of plans for us this week?' she asked.

'No. We just run the event. Carry on as normal.'

'OK, well, we need to visit the Copthorne & Brookes office, see Peters about the programme and pick up the work permits and all the rest of the papers they've got.'

'What's going to be happening here whilst we're in town?'

'I've already checked that all our materials are here. The hotel staff have been instructed to bring everything to the conference room, and once we're back from town, I can start setting up. I've got help coming in from tomorrow, so today is just really ensuring it's all here and doing as much as we can. Ben knows what he's got to do with all the screens, displays and audio-visual equipment. I've told him everything I need doing and he'll make a start whilst we're around. It's a relief to have him here. He's happy to give me a hand.'

Ash said nothing, but gave Dawn a sideways glance that caused her to blush as she carried on talking without missing a beat.

'I'll double-check that the banqueting team know what they're doing and I'll meet you in reception in, say, fifteen minutes. We can stroll into Hamilton together. I've also got to drop the master copy of the documentation in at the printers, once we get some missing bits from Mike Peters. That's if he's pulled his finger out to get hold of them.'

'Peters is expecting us?'

'Oh, yes, I even rang the office to confirm.'

*　　　*　　　*

How Ash wished he could have sent Dawn on her own to see Copthorne & Brookes, but that wasn't fair and, before he knew it, they were sitting with Peters.

'I'm very well organised this year. Harriet helped me get all the paperwork ready for you.'

'Harriet? I'd heard she was on the island. What's she up to these days?' Ash asked, in mock innocence.

'She's on the board of a couple of companies for me and she runs a Chinese import/export business as well. She's a real entrepreneur.'

'As well as your personal assistant, Mr Peters?' Dawn asked.

'She knows this event, so it made sense. Good all round I would have thought. Let's put petty differences aside, at least for this week, shall we? Incidentally, we'd like you to come to a pirate party on Hawkins Island tonight, Dawn. It's informal – you can wear pirate fancy dress if you're daring enough. It'll be a chance for you to escape that boss of yours – sorry, Ash – and let your hair down. He won't mind. It's an important reinsurance do and I've got a ticket for you. A few of this week's speakers might be there, so Ashbury Events should show its face. The party boat leaves Albuoys Point at six this evening and I'll expect you to be on it,' Peters said, as he handed over the ticket to Dawn who took it reluctantly.

They then ran through the programme for the week, getting through it very quickly. All the paperwork was in order, which speeded things up.

Only one aspect concerned Peters.

'I don't want Doug Bonsall at the speakers' party at Selwyn's house tomorrow night.'

'He's always come in the past, Mike and is covering the event for us again this year. He also gets on very well with Selwyn, whose first question is always, "Is Doug here?"'

'Well keep him away from me. And that goes for Dorian Miller and that computer con-artist girlfriend of his, or is it of Doug's? I can't keep up. I don't like the pair of them either.'

'I'm sure they'll all be happy to give you a wide berth, Mike,' Ash replied, 'but Dorian is an important speaker.'

'Important?' sneered Peters. 'Who cares about all that cultural crap. It's only purpose is to keep the wives happy.'

'The partners' programme is actually very popular,' said Dawn indignantly. 'Fifty are registered for the Dock-yard visit.'

'Well, isn't that just grand.'

'I hope the weather holds for the week,' said Ash, 'the

forecasts are predicting storms and a possible hurricane.'

'That's nonsense. We go by Wallace and his shark-oil barometer. Never wrong. It's clear at the moment, so the weather should be good for the cocktail party at least. It might get stormy by the end of the week, so brace yourselves.'

*   *   *

Dawn only agreed to go to the pirate party when Ash said she could take Ben Sanchez with her.

Whilst waiting for the conference documentation to be printed at a copyshop around the corner from Copthorne House, they had a coffee and then found a shop selling fancy dress. Once they had rummaged through the masses of American-inspired Halloween tat that the shop had on display, Dawn found a couple of suitable outfits for her and Ben.

'The things we have to do to keep clients happy, eh?' said Ash as they took a taxi back to the hotel. 'Let's hope you have a fun evening. It might make up for the boring time we'll have this afternoon doing the set-up.'

*   *   *

The party went badly for Dawn and Ben. In that respect, it matched Ash's evening with Dorian, which didn't end well either.

Dawn, having persuaded Ben to go with her, enjoyed the lively atmosphere when they first arrived, and talked to a few of the speakers that she knew.

When Harriet Hall arrived, things took a turn for the worse. Harriet insisted on plying Dawn with glass after glass of Strawberry Daiquiri and dripped poison in her ear about working at Ashbury Events.

'You'll get no career development you know ... You'll get discarded, just like that ... Why don't you come out here for a while and run conferences for Copthorne & Brookes? ... You could set up on your own, even in London ... Do you have copies of all the mailing lists? ... What's your notice period? ... What do you know about Doug Bonsall? ... Is Beatrice Goode actually any good with computers?'

The incessant drone of Harriet's Sloaney voice, the loud carnival music, the mad pirate outfits around her and the wild display of a troupe of Gombay dancers all made Dawn feel slightly queasy. It was like a variation on the Tahitian voodoo sequence in a Bond film, with its cacophonous sound of drums and whistles. It eventually made Dawn feel grim enough to insist Ben took her back to the hotel, where she promptly passed out on her bed.

Ben rang Ash.

'Sorry to bother you, Ash, but I think Dawn's drinks may have been spiked this evening. Can you come over?'

When his phone rang, Ash was trying to read calmly on his balcony, sipping a large rum. He was slowly recovering from having told Dorian that his girlfriend was playing fast and loose, not just with Doug, but possibly also with Gavin.

Earlier, Ash had joined Dorian for a meal in the courtyard of The Chancery Wine Bar, just off Front Street. The sound of tree frogs was all he was left with when Dorian stormed off in the middle of eating his main course. Ash had stayed on, mostly staring at the underside of his table's Cinzano umbrella or at the white gravel on the ground. The heartache and betrayal Ash had seen in Dorian's eyes made him glad of his own settled home life with a wife he could trust.

Ben was wild-eyed and looked very anxious – and faintly ridiculous in his Long John Silver costume – when he opened the door to Ash.

'She's flaked out on the bed, Ash. Should we call a doctor? She can't have had that much to drink.'

'Were you drinking the same? Who got her drinks for her?'

'That Harriet Hall woman made a beeline for Dawn and got her daiquiri after daiquiri whilst Mike Peters took me off to the bar for a Pirate Punch where he proceeded to bore me silly about how Ashbury Events always cock up the slides speakers use.'

'What's going on?'

It was Dawn, drowsily responding to the two men talking.

'Ah, thank goodness for that,' said Ben. 'You've been dead to the world. We thought you might have been drugged or something. I had to manhandle you back to the room.'

'God, how embarrassing, but why are *you* here, Ash?'

'Ben was worried and he knows what we're up against in Peters and Harriet. He thinks your drinks might have been spiked and he's called on my medical expertise for a second opinion.'

'Ugh. This is getting tacky. I'm alright, guys. A bit the worse for wear. Get over it. Those Strawberry Daiquiris went straight to my head. I haven't been drugged. Harriet was so annoying tonight and when my head started spin-ning from tiredness, boredom, booze and jet lag, I just had to get off that damn island.'

'We came back with some of the other guests and the boat dropped us off at the hotel dock. I only just managed to get you up to your room,' said Ben. 'Sorry, I just got a bit worried about you, that's all.'

'Look, fellas, I just need to strip off this ridiculous pirate outfit and get some sleep. Ben, you should heave ho and do the same. I need to sort myself out, otherwise

I won't be in a fit state to run the show tomorrow.'

Ash and Ben left at the same time, although Ash caught sight of Ben blowing Dawn a kiss on the way out.

As the two men walked to the lift, Ash said, 'Nice pirate get-up, Ben.'

'Oh yes, I'd forgotten how ridiculous I look.'

'By the way, how did you get on with Merino and his goons today?'

'Actually, they're a great bunch. Some brilliant stories, and I think they might use me in the UK if I play my cards right. I even helped them bug a few hotel rooms. Oops, I shouldn't have said that, should I?'

'Not if you want to work undercover again, Ben, no. But, I forgot to ask you, how did you get on this afternoon with all the technical side of the conference?'

'All set up, all in place. You were there, Ash, you saw Dawn playing a blinder bossing us all around and once we'd done our thing, we all mucked in to get everything ready. Tomorrow should be a doddle.'

15.

TUESDAY

The registration for the Bermuda Biennial Reinsurance Conference started at two-thirty in the afternoon and Ashbury Events were totally ready when the first delegates dropped by at their reception desk.

Dawn and Ben had done a great job. The display signs were attractive and effective and Ash felt proud of the way it all looked.

He was pleased that Copthorne & Brookes never bothered to send anyone along to the opening afternoon, preferring to welcome the speakers in their own way at the first night cocktail party they held at Selwyn Brookes's house on Point Shares.

Perhaps unsurprisingly, Eddie Wilkins and Carey Merino arrived at the same time to register as delegates. They liked Ash's joke, as he handed Merino his badge with the false name 'J E Dyson'. 'That's J Edgar Dyson,' Ash said, 'because not everyone can be a Hoover.' Merino winced and Wilkins winked as Ash took them both out onto the terrace to have tea and a chat.

'I've been telling Eddie, that it's all low key this week,' Merino said. 'Surveillance is the name of the game for the next few days. We've got enough of the paperwork we need for the case, but we want to see the Peters scam in operation to confirm what we think we know and get some decent further evidence of his fraudulent activity. Eddie and his colleague on the island have given me some nuggets of pure gold in intelligence terms, and now you guys must leave us to it.'

'Actually,' Ash said, 'the only thing that concerns me at the moment is the fallout caused by Beatrice Goode. Eddie, I don't know who knows what about her and you, or what Doug Bonsall and Dorian Miller know, and that's without the Gavin Boatwright connection.'

'Gavin Boatwright?' said Wilkins. 'Who the hell is he?'

Carey Merino and Ash looked at each other. Neither knew quite what to say.

'Beatrice works for you, right?' Merino said to Wilkins.

'She's an associate, not an employee. More freelance than wage slave,' he replied.

'With emphasis on the freelance,' said Ash. 'Maybe you should have a chat with her and get a clearer idea of what she's playing at.'

'What do you mean? She's very professional at what

she does,' Wilkins said.

'She's a pro alright,' Merino said, turning to face the sea, 'but if we're not careful, something like this, if it blows up in our faces, could jeopardise our whole operation. Get it quietly sorted out and limit the damage.'

'You and Eddie should come to the cocktail party this evening. All the speakers will be there,' said Ash, looking at Merino to indicate that these would include his brother Tony from Lehman Brothers. 'As Dorian is a speaker, he'll take Bee as his plus one, and Doug will be there to cover the event for *The Bugle*. You two can come as my guests.'

'So, I finally get to come to *the* famous cocktail party where there'll be some real pros,' said Wilkins, pointedly, as Ash and Merino looked sideways at each other in despair.

'We can observe how Mike Peters, his wife and Harriet Hall work the room if we keep our wits about us,' said Merino, 'it'll all help complete the picture we need.'

*   *   *

Dawn, Ben and Ash shared a taxi from the Hamilton Princess to Selwyn Brookes's home. Ash described the house for them on the way there, as he was the only one who had been to it before.

'It's right by the sea. We'll be outside on the terrace overlooking the garden that slopes down to its own dock. There'll be hundreds of twinkly lights in the trees as well as in the various gazebos dotted around. Flaming torches will light the way down to the water's edge. The house is big and it fits in with designs perfected by a long-dead local architect, Wil Onions, if you can believe that name,' Ash said, sensing he was droning on.

After a few moments' silence, he added, 'Anyway, you can see for yourself, can't you, we're here now.'

*   *   *

They were no sooner in the very large entrance hall – being offered champagne off silver salvers by women in high heels, short skirts, tiny white aprons and revealing tops – than Ash was nobbled by Selwyn Brookes himself, who was loitering near the front door.

'Are these girls serving the drinks part of your team, Mr Ash? My wife had to go and lie down with palpitations at the thought of the damage their stilettos will do to our ancient cedar floors. I must say they look more like hookers from Seventh Avenue to me.'

'I wouldn't know, Mr Brookes. You should ask your Mr Peters. He lays them on.'

'I thought you lot did all the catering for this do of ours,' said Selwyn Brookes, gesturing at Ash, Dawn and Ben.

'Oh no, it's all been organised by Peters and his new partner in crime, Harriet Hall. Take it up with them if you have any concerns. I'm a guest in your wonderful home, along with everyone else,' Ash replied.

'Peters, you say. Whatever next? I'll have to have a word with Wallace about all this when he shows. Never mind, is your friend Doug from *The Bugle* here yet?'

*   *   *

Ash, Dawn and Ben formed a wallflower trio, largely ignored by everyone, as if a decree had been issued by Copthorne & Brookes that anyone being friendly to Ashbury Events would be sacked on the spot.

Fortunately, a few of the speakers can't have received the memo as they came and chatted quite openly with them, much to Peters's annoyance as he had to either come over himself, or send Harriet over to 'rescue' the speaker concerned on the grounds that so and so was 'simply dying' to meet them.

Tony Merino, the star guest from Lehman Brothers, entered into the game and enjoyed himself by sending first Peters, then Harriet and finally Wallace Copthorne away and saying he would join them later.

Carey Merino sidled over and asked for the key players to be pointed out to him. Meanwhile, Dawn and Ben wandered off in search of canapés.

'New York must be out of working girls judging by the waitresses on display here tonight,' was Carey Merino's observation to his brother and Ash. 'The rumour about what goes on at these parties is true then. I can see that speaker in the corner leaning over to whisper something in that girl's ear.'

'His room number, presumably,' said Tony Merino. 'Some people think Lehman Brothers does the same thing, but not on my watch, I can tell you. Pity I can't warn the guy.'

'No, Tony, I need him to take the bait – especially him, he's a complete shyster,' said Carey Merino.

'And all along I thought he was an eminent director of a State Insurance Department,' said Ash.

*   *   *

Ash excused himself and, after circulating and networking as much as he could enjoyably do, he sought out Ben and Dawn who were leaning on the stone balustrade of the terrace and looking out over Hamilton Sound. You could see the bobbing lights of various small craft criss-crossing the harbour and the starry lights of the elegant homes around the water's edge.

As he approached, there was an almighty commotion down by the dock and shouts and screams echoed up to the house.

Ash saw Dorian running up the stairs of the house and tried unsuccessfully to stop him.

Eddie Wilkins came lumbering after him and Ash asked, 'What the hell is going on?'

'It was Dorian. He launched himself at Doug and pushed him into the sea. He's being fished out now.'

A nearby Mike Peters heard all this.

'Seems like Ashbury Events has a few loose cannons, eh, Ash? Can't hold their liquor or can't keep hold of their women. Selwyn and Wallace won't be impressed with this sort of behaviour.'

Dawn put an arm on Ash's and he managed to reply calmly, 'If anything, Mike, it seems to go with the general tenor of the evening. But I know Dorian, there's bound to be an innocent explanation.'

As Peters wandered off, Wilkins came back to their group.

'Lost him. He must have jumped into an arriving cab

and taken it. There's no sign of him out on the road. I'd better go and see how Bee is getting on.'

'I'll come with you,' said Ash. 'You two should feel free to leave,' he added to Dawn and Ben. 'I'll see you bright and early tomorrow for the start of the conference. Can't wait!'

*   *   *

'We all met at Oxford Beaches for a drink before we came over for the party,' Wilkins explained on the walk down the steps to the dock. 'Doug and Dorian had invites and Bee came as Dorian's guest.'

'What led to the fracas?'

'We all had a heart to heart over drinks – everything out in the open, cards on the table. Bee apologised to Doug and Dorian for the way she's behaved and for not telling them she was working with me as well as Cogence. On the way over, we shared a cab and Bee apologised to me for holding back about new clients. She said she'd fill me in properly when we had the chance, but that she was onto something even bigger than Mike Peters.'

'What was the atmosphere like between Dorian and Doug?'

'Although they didn't talk much in the cab, I thought Dorian had taken it all pretty well, but he must have seethed about it on the way over. When we arrived, Bee said we should take a look at the water, so we all strolled down. Dorian suddenly said to Doug, "You're as immoral as any of the shits you investigate." At least I think that's what he said. The next thing, Doug was in the water, Bee was screaming and everyone nearby was shouting man overboard before they rallied round and started to haul Doug ashore using the lifebuoy someone threw in after him.'

By the time Wilkins and Ash arrived at the scene, Doug was sitting on the edge of the dock wall with a towel round his shoulders.

Bee looked distraught.

'I suppose you blame me for all this, Ash, but there's no need to give me such a sanctimonious look,' she said.

'This won't get us anywhere,' Ash replied. 'I suggest you, Doug and Eddie make as quiet an exit as you can. We can't exactly pass this off as an accident given that Mike Peters has already heard what happened, but I'll play it down as much as I can.'

'Don't worry, Ash, I won't be writing this up in *The Bugle*,' said Doug.

*　　*　　*

When Ash sought out Selwyn Brookes, he found him with Wallace Copthorne and Mike Peters.

'I'm sorry about that little commotion, gentlemen,' he said. 'Seems like a misunderstanding – a bit of jostling and a loss of footing put Doug in the drink.'

'Not good, Mr Ash, and not the image we want to present at the home of one of our distinguished partners. Dorian Miller is your man, isn't he? You'd better read him the riot act.'

'Come, come, Wallace,' interjected Brookes. 'We've had worse than that. Don't you remember when our entire audit team dived off the dock naked at one of the firm's summer parties?'

Despite that kindly response, which raised his spirits slightly, Ash thought he'd better be off, so he thanked them for their hospitality.

Smirking at the discomfort caused by the incident, Peters followed Ash out.

'Don't worry, Ash, these things happen. Boys will be boys and all that. By the way, was that guy Eddie Wilkins with Dorian, Bee and Doug?'

'I don't think so.'

'Then how did he get in?'

Take the rap, Ash, he told himself. Doug has been in enough deep water for one night.

'I think I might have suggested he came as I knew he'd been talking to you about doing some reinsurance business.'

'Do I really need to remind you that it's a speakers' cocktail party and not for any old hangers-on? See you tomorrow. Goodnight, Ash.'

16.

The conference's formal opening session went very well. The Premier officially welcomed the delegates, having himself been introduced by the sycophantic words of the chairman, Wallace Copthorne:

> *My old friend, Sir Dennis Bird, is once again the special guest of Copthorne & Brookes. He has spared time from his busy schedule to be with us today and show how highly he regards this event and Bermuda's reinsurance industry. We pride ourselves that a man of his business background wants to recognise the contribution we all make to the safety and welfare of the world. He has asked me in particular to thank the catastrophe reinsurance companies represented here at this Bermuda Biennial for the work we do helping the United States rebuild areas devastated by natural and man-made disasters. I*

now hand you over to Sir Dennis Bird, KBE who will open our conference and explain the latest legislation he has personally introduced to make sure Bermuda remains at the forefront of the world of finance. Ladies and gentlemen, Sir Dennis Bird.

This closeness to government always put Wallace Copthorne in a good mood and even Ashbury Events staff were treated relatively cordially by him throughout the day.

Specialist speakers addressed the burning issues in the London and US markets as well as emerging markets like the Asia Pacific basin, China and Eastern Europe. A fun day, in other words, if you like that sort of thing.

Harriet had arrived with Peters in the morning and Ash was in the difficult position of not being able to prevent her staying throughout. He guessed it played into Carey Merino's hands so that enabled him to grin and bear it.

'Where's that useless journalist of yours, Ash?' Peters asked during the short break after Sir Dennis Bird had opened proceedings. 'It's lucky Harriet is here to take the photos and she can write up something suitable for *The Bugle* to use. Your man Bonsall put on quite a show last night and now he's a no-show here today. He's turning that newspaper into *The Royal Bungle*. What a berk! You can't half pick 'em.'

Peters gave no time for Ash to reply as he walked off with Harriet Hall.

*　　　*　　　*

The break-out sessions during the day were what really intrigued Ash and Carey Merino. Harriet Hall was on hand throughout, to conspicuously approach various delegates and speakers and corral them into a smaller room that had been set up for group discussions with Mike Peters acting as Chair.

At the end of the first morning break, Ash and Carey Merino lingered over their coffee and pastries, seeing their plans unfold.

'We've got that room covered, Ash, don't worry. If we get anything like the stuff we got overnight from the bedrooms we bugged, we really are in business. These dudes think they are savvy businessmen yet they spill their guts to girls they've just met like they're in confession and talking to their priests.'

'Any confessions of a serial fraudster?'

'My content analysis boys are on the case with the tapes as we speak. The overnight word was that piling money into the Bermuda Bond because of spectacular returns is a turn on for these guys. Let's hope the girls found it as stimulating.'

*　　　*　　　*

At lunch, Ash ducked out and tried to call Doug at *The Bugle*, but the newspaper's receptionist told him that he was out covering an event at the Hamilton Princess.

Ash then tried Dorian, who was, his assistant said, conducting a tour of the Dockyard museum with a group of Chinese businessmen.

Wilkins was hob-nobbing with a group of insurance insolvency practitioners, veterans of the KWELM never-ending run-off, when Ash located him.

'Sorry to interrupt, Eddie, but do you know where I might find Bee?'

'Can't help, Ash. She's working with one of her IT clients today. I don't know which. Maybe JP Margeson, but she could be over at Oxford Beaches. Have you tried there?'

Ash tried Gavin Boatwright at his hotel.

'No, Ash, Beatrice *was* due here today, but left a message to say she couldn't make it and that I should ask Dorian the reason why. When I challenged him, he said he'd made a bit of a fool of himself with Doug and that he and Bee had split up.'

Ash sought out Carey Merino who was having a sandwich with Ben and his team.

'I'm concerned,' Ash said. 'I can't track down Doug

... and Bee seems to have gone AWOL. Am I getting paranoid?'

'Well, after last night, the implication might be that they're together somewhere,' said Ben.

'Maybe, but it's odd that Doug didn't get himself here today. I'm going to speak to his editor and flag this up, even if it gets Doug into trouble,' Ash replied.

'OK,' said Merino, 'I'll speak to Scott Roberts. He's actually working with us on this Peters investigation and can visit Doug and Bee's home addresses if you like.'

*   *   *

There was no news on Doug or Bee throughout the afternoon. At the three-thirty tea break, Merino reported back on his chat with the Bermudian police and their undertaking to check things out. Shortly after, a call came through from Dorian on the conference desk telephone.

'Hi, Ash! I'm so sorry about last night. Everything just boiled over. It's not like me at all. I feel a complete idiot for behaving like that. The trouble is, I hadn't seen what was happening under my nose. In the cab on the way to the party, I looked back and could see a pattern emerging in Bee's behaviour. I'm a historian, Ash, and events only make any sense in retrospect. It finally dawned on me what a dupe I'd been and I lashed out at Doug. I can't believe I did what I did.'

'Look, don't worry about that. Just carry on and it will get sorted out, although you should know that Doug didn't come to the opening session today and I'm more than a bit concerned.'

'I've messed up, Ash. Give me a day or so to get over this and I'll speak to him.'

'I don't suppose you've heard from Bee, have you, Dorian?'

'No. I think that ship has sailed.'

'I really wouldn't know about that. Who knows what'll happen next. But listen, whilst I've got you, are you going to come to the party at the Yacht Club tonight?'

'Do you think I should?'

'I think you must – show your face, at least.'

*   *   *

Usually, for Ash, the highlight of the party at the Royal Bermuda Yacht Club was watching the hosts – the local law firm of Lemon, Lockhart & White – try to outmanoeuvre Copthorne & Brookes by power-flirting with the delegates who weren't already clients.

So that they could easily be picked out by potential clients, the partners of the prestigious law firm all wore identical outfits of matching yellow Bermuda shorts, short-sleeved yellow shirts, and yellow knee-length socks.

'What they wear at these functions must be written into the partnership agreement,' Ash said, addressing Dawn, Ben and Carey Merino, who were standing with him as they listened to Raymond White, the senior partner, make his speech. He thanked everyone for coming and, stating the obvious, pointed out that guests should feel free to engage with the representatives of his firm by seeking out the men in yellow.

Dawn and Ash mingled with the conference delegates and speakers, chatting to the friendlier ones, whilst Ben headed outside to enjoy a drink and take in the views of the harbour.

'Thanks, Mr White, for hosting this wonderful event for us again,' Dawn managed to say before he patted her on the arm with a 'Don't mention it' as he looked over her shoulder for a more deserving recipient of his attention, someone with a bigger potential client appeal.

'Just before you circulate, Raymond,' Ash said, 'I believe Beatrice Goode has been doing some computer work for you. Is she here tonight, do you know?'

'I haven't seen her and she didn't come in today for an important update on her Y2K compliance work. Still, she's freelance, so I suppose that's what she thinks she can do. I wasn't pleased. You can tell her that if you see her before I do. Now, if you don't mind.'

As Raymond White went off to cast his net elsewhere, Dorian tapped Ash on the shoulder.

'It's a very penitent me,' he said. 'Can we have a word?'

Ash and Dorian each took a glass of the Yacht Club's famous tiki-style cocktail from a passing waiter, and went outside onto the terrace.

*   *   *

Unusually, the real highlight of this year's Lemon, Lockhart & White cocktail party at the one hundred and fifty-year-old Royal Bermuda Yacht Club, was the arrival of the police in the form of two uniformed officers.

They were standing at the desk being used to check off the list of party attendees, and Dawn went over to find out what was happening.

'We're here to have a word with Dorian Miller. Can you point him out to us?'

Noticing that the presence of the officers was already attracting attention, Dawn said, 'I think it would be better if I fetch him and perhaps meet you in the lobby.'

They agreed and left the main room, but not before

everybody had noticed them. All eyes were then on Dawn as she went out to the terrace and reappeared with Ash and Dorian, leading them out to the waiting police.

When Ash came back into the party on his own, people carried on chatting and drinking as if nothing had happened and pretended they hadn't been distracted. Except, that is, for Mike Peters.

'What on earth is going on, Ash? First, last night's little display, and now this.'

'It's something and nothing,' Ash replied. 'You might as well know that Doug Bonsall and Beatrice Goode are missing and the police are trying to track them down. It's no big deal. No scandal. Sorry to disappoint you.'

'You never disappoint us, Ash. You live up to the gaffe-prone image we're forming of you. What next? This week is turning out to be a bit of an Ashbury Events soap opera, isn't it?'

At this point, Dawn, Ben and Merino joined them, which only encouraged Peters and his taunting.

'Whilst we're at it, Ash, you should cancel that golf tournament tomorrow and move the gala dinner inside. Our shark oil is telling us a storm is brewing and the weather maps say it will hit us mid-afternoon. Your week is a bit of a wash-out, isn't it?'

Peters went off, full of himself, leaving Ash to explain to the others.

'They've taken Dorian off to help with their enquiries into the disappearance of Doug and Bee. I can't believe it. They know all about what happened last night.'

'That might be down to me, Ash,' said Merino.

Dawn tried to offer some comfort.

'Well, if the worst comes to the worst and, God forbid they keep Dorian in, don't worry about the partners' programme. I always ask presenters to nominate a deputy and we've got Dorian's boss as understudy for tomorrow. We can take a weather check and cancel the golf. Nobody will mind. And Elbow Beach can accommodate the dinner inside, no trouble at all. They're used to it with the weather here.'

'Thanks, Dawn. I'm glad you're able to focus on the show going on, but whatever next?'

Merino scratched his chin before commenting.

'If it's any consolation, Ash, I've got to hand it to you. I feared the worst, but all the goings-on of last night and today act as a wonderful smokescreen to hide my operation. And Peters is looking really pleased with himself. That's an added bonus. Smug and over-confident, just as we need him to be! It keeps him off guard – as if nobody is looking at him. Perfect. Please tell me you planned it all? At this rate, I'm going to have to make you agent of the month.'

'It may disguise *your* operation, Carey, but it puts Ashbury Events under a microscope,' said Ash. 'I'm going to have to go to the police station and see what's going on with Dorian. I'll have to help him. He may need a lawyer and I doubt if any of the clowns here in yellow would be of any use unless Dorian had some money to hide.'

'If I can help, I'll meet you there, Ash, but best not leave together,' said Merino. 'I'll stay and chat with Dawn and Ben for a while.'

17.

THURSDAY

The clouds darkened throughout the morning. At first a shower, then came the really heavy rain which started in earnest at around eleven o'clock.

The golf was officially cancelled.

The partners' programme was switched to being a lecture in the first-floor tea room of the Hamilton Princess, with a sandwich lunch, all hosted by the Director of the Royal Naval Dockyard.

The weather was to be at its worst during the day, easing off towards the evening for the gala dinner, which was something at least.

At the first coffee break, Mike Peters, with Harriet Hall in tow, arrived for the day and sought Ash out.

'What extramural entertainment have you got lined up for us today, Ash?'

'Because of the weather –'

'I've heard that,' Peters butted in, 'and, as you may not know, Wallace, today's chairman, is going to announce a special reinsurance-related investment symposium this afternoon. We'll then have an extra session on alternative dispute resolution for any delegates interested. I'll say a few words about current investment opportunities here on Bermuda. What would you do without us?'

*   *   *

Dorian remained in custody. Ash and Carey had failed to get him released the night before as Scott Roberts had been more worried about Doug's disappearance than feeling sorry for the man who'd attacked him. The police had also refused to entertain the possibility that Peters might have had anything to do with it.

'You're playing the same broken record as Doug, Mr Ash. This has nothing to do with Peters and no, we're not going to speak to him about it,' was how Scott Roberts had put it. 'We're keeping Mr Miller in overnight – he can see a lawyer in the morning when we question him again.'

So much for police interrogation techniques – they'd linked the alleged assault on Tuesday evening with the subsequent disappearance of Doug and Bee and, by putting two and two together, they'd made – for Dorian – the worst possible four.

Later that morning, Carey found out that lawyers had been retained on Dorian's behalf by the Dockyard and Dorian was released on bail, retreating back to Oxford Beaches from where he contacted Ash.

'They think I might have bumped them both off so I could be re-arrested at any time. I think they've only let me go to see what I do. I bet this line is tapped. So, for the record, I've nothing whatsoever to do with the disappearance of Doug and Bee. It must be related to what the pair of them were working on. Someone's found out that they dug up too much dirt and has done something to eliminate the threat that their information posed.'

'Did you tell the police about the murdered banker?'

'Of course I did, but all they were interested in was my jealousy of Doug and Bee's affair. They obviously feel that since I attacked Doug at the cocktail party, I'm capable of anything.'

'How were you treated?'

'I've no complaints on that score, Ash, and I'm not just saying that for the benefit of whoever else may or may not be listening. What's far worse than being incarcerated, as far as I'm concerned, is that I'm simply not being believed. You've no idea what that feels like. When somebody thinks you're lying and you can't seem to shake their view, you feel the same rage as when you know someone is lying to you and they won't admit it. So I can see where they're coming from.'

'What has the Dockyard said about things?'

'I'm out of a job, Ash, they've made that plain.'

'But you're not guilty of anything.'

'Whichever way you look at it, it's gross misconduct in their view, not helped by the fact that the Director was pissed off about having to take my slot at the conference. Sorry about that, by the way.'

'Don't worry. Everything's fine. Have a rest, Dorian, and I'll come and see you later. I've got the gala dinner this evening, but I'll come over when I can.'

*   *   *

Ash then managed to find Wilkins. He didn't have to look far. He found him trying to chat up Dawn by the conference reception desk. Some things don't change, he thought.

'Eddie, can I have a quiet word with you, please?' Ash said. 'What happened to you, Doug and Bee after the party?'

'Doug was chatting to Mrs Peters, who was fussing over him with towels, when Bee and I decided to leave at the same time. I wanted to walk back to the hotel, as it was such a nice evening – the calm before the storm as it turns out. Doug stayed to dry off and Bee said she had some files to examine so she wanted to go her own separate way. Apparently, she's got back-up copies of all her papers locked in the safe at *The Bugle*'s offices so she didn't want to fall out with Doug.'

'You told me that Bee was working on something "bigger than Peters". What was that?'

'I did ask her before I left last night. She's gained access to the computer system at Oxford Beaches and it seems that Gavin has had his fingers in lots of pies. Bee's busy putting together all the pieces of a fiendishly complicated jigsaw. I told her to be careful but she claims to have the complete trust of Gavin who dotes on her.'

'Do you think she's in some kind of relationship with him?'

'Wouldn't surprise me. It's how she seems to operate.'

'It's a dangerous game, isn't it? Spying on someone you're sleeping with.'

'Haven't you heard of Mata Hari, Ash?'

'Yes, I have. And look what happened to her.'

'Come on, Ash. For my money, I still think Bee and Doug are holed up somewhere. I could tell on Tuesday evening there's a heck of a spark between the two of them – no offence to your old pal Dorian.'

'Now the golf's been cancelled, I'm going out to Oxford Beaches to see Dorian this afternoon and I'll report back. Now I'm worried about Bee *and* Doug.'

'You're going out in this weather?' Wilkins said, gazing at the rain beating against the windows of the hotel. 'Let me know if you need me to do anything – preferably indoors, if you don't mind.'

'I'm sure the rain will ease later in time for the gala dinner. Are you coming this evening?'

'You bet, it's part of the ticket price.'

'Which you didn't pay for!'

'You know me, Ash! See you later.'

*　　*　　*

After lunch, Ash managed to get a cab out to Oxford Beaches, but only because the driver lived at Daniel's Head and it was on his way home.

The rain was torrential and progress was slow. When Ash eventually arrived, he dashed in through the hotel's main entrance and asked the receptionist to put him through to Dorian's room.

'He's not there, Mr Ash.'

It was Gavin Boatwright who came out of the little office behind reception to give Ash this piece of news.

'I'm afraid you've missed your friend. He's just been

re-arrested by the police, I'm afraid.'

'Why? On what grounds?'

'I'm sorry, but I had to inform them that he'd confessed to the abduction of Miss Goode, but wouldn't tell me what he'd done with her. Naturally, I felt he should explain himself to the police.'

'I don't believe it.'

'What don't you believe?'

'That Dorian would do a thing like that.'

'Like confess? Or like abduction? All I can tell you is that, in my experience, we never really know people – especially those close to us.'

'I thought Dorian was a friend of yours, Gavin. You don't seem to care about him at all.'

'He *is* a friend. I'm glad he's got lawyers working for him and hope he can prove his innocence. But, you know, Ash, we have a duty to obey the law and that goes for our friends as well as our enemies. Now, I'm sorry you've had a wasted journey. Stay here and dry off and let's try and get you a cab,' Boatwright said as he clicked his fingers at the receptionist. 'I've got to do the rounds and check there are no leaks anywhere. Do help yourself to the complimentary drinks and biscuits whilst you wait.'

Ash did just that and, eventually, the receptionist managed to speak to the only taxi firm that was willing to send a cab out to Oxford Beaches in spite of the weather.

'I'm sorry about Mr Miller,' the receptionist said to Ash as he sat in one of the rattan peacock chairs opposite her desk. 'He's a really nice man. I can't believe this of him.'

'Did you know Beatrice Goode, the woman who has vanished into thin air?'

'Yes, I did. I shouldn't say this, but she was awfully friendly with Mr B as well as Mr Miller – more so, if anything. She has been here rather a lot recently.'

'Have you seen her in the last couple of days?'

'I thought I saw her arrive late on Tuesday evening and make her way to Mr B's bungalow, but the next morning he made a big thing about her not turning up. I said I'd seen her the night before but he was insistent I was mistaken and since then he's been behaving very oddly. He took the tender out to his yacht a few times yesterday and again this morning before the sea got too rough. It looks to me like he's getting ready to go on a trip as soon as the storm passes as he keeps checking the weather.'

'How often does he go out on the yacht?'

'He usually sets off in the evening and returns the next day. Says he enjoys sailing by the stars and it's true, he really does love the sea. He and Mr Miller were always talking about sailing and naval history.'

'What are you two gossiping about?'

It was a very wet Gavin Boatwright coming back into the hotel.

'Ash, your cab's here. You can't keep it waiting. I don't want the hotel getting a bad reputation. We're out on a limb here as it is, without being even more cut off because we abuse the local taxi service.'

*   *   *

Having missed Dorian at Oxford Beaches, Ash was back at the Hamilton Princess long before he'd expected. He sought out Carey Merino and found him chewing the fat with Ben, who made his excuses as he needed to check on the recordings being made in the various rooms.

Ash explained to Merino what had happened at Oxford Beaches and shared a theory he'd explored in his mind on the cab journey back.

'They've arrested Dorian again. Boatwright dropped him in it by telling the police Dorian had confessed to abducting Bee.'

'Well, you can't blame the police, Ash. What do you expect them to do?' Merino said.

'I know, I know. But Boatwright was behaving strangely and the receptionist seemed to think he was getting ready for a yacht trip once the bad weather is over. What if he's got Bee on board his yacht and is blaming Dorian to cover himself?'

'I thought you just wanted to run conferences, Ash.

Now you're turning all Columbo on me.'

'How can we get the police out to search Boatwright's yacht – *and* his hotel for that matter?'

'Bee said that Boatwright had some kind of past life in drugs and money laundering.'

'Doug said that as well.'

'How sure are you that the yacht has something to do with Bee's disappearance?' Merino asked.

'Stronger than a hunch because the receptionist thinks she saw Bee at the hotel late on Tuesday evening, so that would be the last sighting of her, after the Copthorne & Brookes cocktail party. Boatwright mostly goes out for overnight trips on his yacht. Where to? There's only ocean for miles and miles.'

'That's what sailors do, Ash. But, just to play ball with you and go along with your theory, how about this as an idea? Why don't I ring Scott Roberts and say I've had a tip off from the DEA in Miami that Boatwright is doing some drug running from his yacht and planning a rendezvous for this evening when the storm has passed. Let's see what they say. Do we know for sure Boatwright is involved in drugs?'

'Affirmative,' said Ash.

'You've seen too many films,' Merino replied.

*   *   *

'OK, Ash,' said Merino, after he'd made the call. 'The police say that they can't do anything before eight o'clock this evening as the sea is too choppy. It might be OK after that, but they're making no promises. They'll be using a small boat so can only do a search if Boatwright's yacht is fairly close to the shore – before he sets sail in other words. They'll also send a couple of men out to the hotel at around the same time.'

'What do *we* do?'

'We go out to Oxford Beaches, of course.'

'What? You and me?'

'Yes, and maybe Wilkins should come too. He works with the woman after all. I'll arrange it with him.'

*   *   *

There was no further news from Dorian and the police refused to let Ash talk to him on the telephone.

Ash could barely concentrate on the gala dinner. The storm had passed and only a light drizzle dampened the occasion.

Elbow Beach looked windswept when Ash arrived and looking out over the terrace to the still wild ocean, he noticed that Club Mickey, the hotel's beach bar, had taken a battering.

Still, inside the Café Lido restaurant, the hotel staff had created an elegant setting for the dinner. Ash's speech of welcome, after the first course of Bermuda fish chowder, contained a few digs at Copthorne & Brookes – good natured, they thought: 'I've worked so long with Wallace Copthorne and Mike Peters, you think they'd have offered me partner status by now ... The only people who always travel first class to Bermuda are insolvency practitioners ... Our distinguished speakers don't come to Bermuda for the speaking fee, so it must be because of the ineffable charm of Wallace Copthorne,' all of which went down rather well with the audience.

As a customary and selfless gesture Ash, Dawn, Ben and all those working on the conference with Ashbury Events were at the worst table in the room, the one by the kitchen. This had the advantage that Ash was able to leave the dinner surreptitiously at seven-thirty with Carey Merino. They met up with Eddie Wilkins outside, who had gamely brought a taxi down to the beachside restaurant to pick them up.

'And I didn't even get to have the starter,' Wilkins said.

'Best do what we've got to do on an empty stomach, guys,' said Merino.

'What are you expecting?' asked Ash.

'The unexpected,' replied Merino.

*　　　*　　　*

They arrived at Oxford Beaches just before eight. By then the rain had stopped completely and the night sky was clear. They told the taxi driver to wait for them.

The same receptionist was on duty.

'Hello again,' said Ash. 'We've arranged to meet Mr Boatwright to see if we can get his help to free Dorian, so we'll go straight along to his room, if that's OK.'

'I've got to call first, I'm afraid,' she said. "Otherwise I'll get the sack.'

'Tell you what,' said Ash. 'Just pretend you never saw us. Tell us which room he's in and we'll surprise him.'

When they knocked on the door, it was flung open by Boatwright, dressed in what can only be described as a nautical get-up – rigged as he was in shorts, deck shoes, and a dark blue waterproof over a light blue sweater. He tried to close the door in their faces when he saw who it was.

'You can't just come here unannounced. Did you go to reception? I'll meet you there.'

Merino had his foot in the door.

'No, we'll come in and have a chat. I'm Carey Merino, FBI, Mr Boatwright, and I think you know Ash here and Eddie Wilkins.'

'What the hell do you want, barging in like this. I'll

call the police. All I have to do is press this panic button,' said Boatwright, walking towards his bed.

'I wouldn't do that if I were you, Gavin. The police are already on their way,' said Ash. 'Why don't you tell us what's happened to Bee?'

'Ask your bloody friend Dorian. He's the one responsible.'

'Let's just relax, shall we,' said Merino. 'For starters, tell us about the boat you've got moored just offshore. Are you planning on taking it out some time soon? It might be nice to take a look at it. That would be a friendly gesture.'

Boatwright turned quickly and, before any of them had a chance to react, produced a small black revolver that he pointed at Merino.

'Don't do anything you'll regret, Boatwright,' said Merino.

'Like offer free accommodation again to Ash's friend, Dorian Miller, you mean?'

'Like with that gun,' said Merino. 'Look at me, look at me. Put it down.'

Boatwright waved the gun in the general direction of all three of them.

'You burst in here. The local police know I have a gun. It's for my protection. I'm acting in self-defence. You're threatening me. I'll shoot unless you let me walk out of here. I'm going to my yacht. You can't stop me or I'll have you charged with assault.'

'The police are on their way, Gavin. Seriously,' said Ash.

'Tell that to the marines. You're bluffing. I'm going to leave. One move from any of you and I'll shoot.'

Wilkins suddenly jumped forward, simultaneously knocking the gun to the floor and head-butting Boatwright in the face, who fell back onto the bed clutching his bleeding nose. Carey Merino pounced on the gun and pointed it at the sprawling figure.

'Nice work, Eddie,' Merino said. 'Couldn't have done it better myself.'

'That's the advantage of being brought up on a council estate in Catford,' Wilkins said, rubbing his sore and bruised forehead, 'but I think I've slightly concussed myself.'

＊   ＊   ＊

When the police arrived they were immediately in contact with officers waiting on their boat near the hotel. After hearing Carey Merino's briefing, they formally arrested and cuffed Gavin Boatwright before searching his room and the rest of the hotel.

The little gathering decamped to reception much to

the astonishment of the receptionist.

'Did you let these people come straight to my room?' Boatwright asked her aggressively.

'That's enough,' said Merino. 'We found your room ourselves. We're that smart.'

*   *   *

Bee's body was found on the yacht. The officers reported that there were marks on her neck indicating that the cause of death was strangulation and the body was stiff and cold. Some guns, rope, extra tarpaulin and large stones were being stored on board. They discovered a large stash of cocaine. There was a large kitbag full of files and paperwork, and the fridge was full of fresh supplies.

The police clearly disbelieved Boatwright's continued insistence that it must have been Dorian who had strangled Bee and dumped her body on his boat. He loudly protested his innocence. 'I've been framed, I've been framed. It was Dorian Miller,' he shouted as he was led away to the police car.

Ash asked the police to release Dorian, but they reminded him that he was actually being held because of the missing Mr Bonsall. Now that the body of Beatrice

Goode had been found, they pointed out, it made the situation worse for Dorian, not better.

Thanking the receptionist, and telling her she'd do well to get the deputy manager to run the hotel for the next few days, Ash took the waiting cab back to Hamilton with Wilkins and Merino, leaving a couple of police officers on site at Oxford Beaches. The taxi driver wore the incredulous expression of a TV addict who'd just finished watching an episode of his favourite detective series.

'Tell Dawn and Ben what's happened,' Ash said to Merino and Wilkins in the taxi, 'you can drop me at the police station and I'll try and see Dorian.'

'We've got to get hold of Bee's files. I assume the police will keep the papers found on the boat,' Wilkins said to Merino.

'We've got to find Doug first, Eddie,' he replied.

'By the way, I'll tell the police that Doug was last seen with Fiona Peters,' said Ash. 'That's right, isn't it, Eddie – can you confirm that, if they ask?'

'Yes. That's what I saw. Given the supposed antagonism between them, she appeared friendly, but she's like that with anything in trousers from what I've seen.'

'Just stick to the facts, Eddie, when you talk to the police. I may need to call you tonight when I'm with them,' Ash said.

'What do you think Boatwright thought he was doing?' Wilkins asked.

'All the evidence points to a plan to take the body out to sea and dump it,' said Merino. 'It remains to be seen whether she was killed on shore or on the boat.'

'If Bee and Doug do have a big fat dossier on Boat-wright, he would have been desperate to get his hands on it. He'd want to destroy any files as well as disposing of the body,' Wilkins said.

'God, what a terrible end for Bee. What on earth will Dorian's reaction to this latest twist be?' Ash sighed and rubbed his brow.

'I'm glad I listened to you and was able to get the police to act,' said Merino. 'Now I can turn my attention back to reeling in Peters and Copthorne. We've got the evidence, I think, but we still need a breakthrough to nail them to the mast.'

'You're forgetting Doug!' Ash sighed again and shook his head. 'They must have had something to do with his disappearance. God, what if he's dead as well?'

18.

FRIDAY

The final day of the conference.

Despite the storm having passed, with the threatened hurricane downgraded and missing the island by some distance, the day was dull and overcast.

Ash was down early to greet Dawn and Ben who were already there on duty when he arrived. Everything was under control.

The last morning was usually a wrap-up session with a panel of speakers reviewing the threats and opportunities facing the reinsurance industry worldwide.

Inevitably, it was chaired every year by Wallace Copthorne and Mike Peters, a double act of two straight men – never a formula for a fun-filled performance. It was, however, what the subject demanded and you couldn't doubt the confidence with which they presented themselves to their audience.

It sickened Ash, who'd left Dorian in a complete state the night before. Utterly destroyed by the news of Bee's death and feeling guilty about the way he'd behaved, he'd immediately taken full responsibility as he'd introduced her to Gavin Boatwright in the first place. He'd said he didn't care any longer if he was released or not. Ash had left him in a very dark place emotionally, looking shattered and defeated.

In complete contrast, Mike Peters arrived full of beans for the final day.

'So, Ash, Gavin Boatwright is now suspect numero uno. The Assistant Commissioner – who incidentally is Wallace's brother-in-law and a great friend of my wife's – well, he says that Beatrice Goode has been murdered. Seems like your friend Dorian Miller is in the clear for that at least, but presumably still in the frame for Doug Bonsall. Pity Bonsall can't do a feature on his own disappearance. A double murder on the island – all in the space of a week. If not the work of one man, perhaps we've got two killers in our midst – Miller and Boatwright – and both of them your friends, Ash. What does that say about Ashbury Events and the risk it now poses of bringing the reputation of Copthorne & Brookes into disrepute? I'd say we've got good grounds for sacking you as our partners in this event and going it alone.'

'Let's see, shall we, Mike. The week isn't over yet. Incidentally,' Ash added, 'your wife was the last person seen talking to Doug.' He wasn't even sure his final remark had been heard as Peters turned and walked away.

*   *   *

Tony and Carey Merino were talking to Ash outside the conference room when the session started.

'I don't think I can listen to Wallace Flopthorne and his sidekick any more,' said Tony Merino, 'and I'm sure the Board of Lehman Brothers would support me. They're insufferable. All week Mike Peters has been trying to bribe me to put more Lehman clients and investments into the Bermuda Bond.'

'That's all they seem to care about,' said Carey Merino. 'The overnight analysis of the tapes of yesterday's session showed them giving an even more blatant sales pitch. They're offering sizeable, double-figure commissions to any firm introducing new investors, and the returns they're promising on the investment are eye-watering.'

'They are, but they say it's because they invest the Bond funds into their own reinsurance firm in the main, which they boast is making profits hand over fist,' said Ash. 'They claim that there's been a huge growth in property catastrophe reinsurance and that premiums are going through the roof. One handout I've seen that was left in the meeting room showed that CaBRe has around sixty different subsidiaries handling reinsured claims in property catastrophe and environmental damage and clean-up business.'

'They do offer a preposterous return on investment,' said Tony Merino. 'Peters is great at selling securities and investments, but he has no moral compass whatsoever. It's as if his heroes are Bernie Cornfeld, Robert Vesco and Marc Rich. Boy, would I like to see the accounts of CaBRe. I never thought anyone would be able to show more creative techniques in accounting than Lehman Brothers. In a way, you have to hand it to them – even if their selling techniques fall foul of every Securities and Exchange Commission regulation.'

'We've got more than that on them, Tony, and, incidentally, the SEC have already been notified,' said Carey Merino.

Tony, leaving Carey and Ash outside, went back into the conference room to show willing and, as he put it, to 'look at Peters and Copthorne and see corruption made flesh'.

'What have you got so far?' Ash asked Carey Merino.

'Charles Ponzi would have been proud of the Bermuda Bond. The link to sleaze with the girls being used as honey traps and the resulting blackmail is a deceitful extra element to the straightforward conning of punters. Both are designed to get investment into the

Bond that offers, they say, sky-high rates of return. They attract gullible investors. You can see how greed begets greed.'

'So in a way, you're saying that the corruption of Peters and Copthorne is matched with the get-rich-quick ambition of investors who deserve to be ripped off.'

'I'm here to investigate law-breakers, not the naïve who still deserve our protection from their own baser instincts, Ash,' Merino replied. 'And, the way that Harriet Hall procures investors is about as immoral a scam as I've seen. She refers to Peters as a "Manager of Fortune" to prospective clients and all the time she's pimping out prostitutes to lure the unsuspecting into a trap. We're going to have a field day just listing their misdemeanours.'

'By the way, Carey, Dawn told me that Peters and Copthorne kept going out of the session yesterday and were deep in conversation in the hotel lobby with Mrs Peters at one point.'

'Yes,' said Merino, 'Ben said the same thing. Fortunately, our guys have come up with an ingenious way of listening to what they say on their radio mics, even if Peters and Copthorne have switched them off. I've told them to do that again this morning.'

'You might be disappointed. Once, when a speaker had accidentally forgotten to switch off *his* radio mic, all his audience heard was the sound of him going to the loo. When he walked back in, all the delegates spontaneously applauded.'

*   *   *

The morning coffee and pastry break was lively with the delegates having the demob-happy spirit that comes at the end of a three-day conference.

Ash went into the conference room to have a word with Ben, who was sitting at the back controlling the lighting, sound and visuals.

'Carey tells me his guys have worked out how to record the radio mics even when the speakers have turned them off,' said Ash.

'That's right. I've learnt quite a few new tricks this week.'

'Heard anything special from the radio mics?'

'We only figured that out yesterday so Carey's guys have been listening this morning to the conversation that Peters and Copthorne were having with Peters's wife yesterday afternoon. That might be interesting.'

'Look, Ben, I'm feeling a bit mischievous. If Peters and Copthorne switch their radio mics off when they leave the room this morning, would you not only be able to listen in, but also play them back over the speakers?'

'Play it live by overriding the off switch, you mean?'

'Precisely.'

'Why would you want to do that if we can record them anyway, Ash?'

'To embarrass them, Ben – call it revenge. If I could inflict a small public humiliation, I'd get some pathetic satisfaction from it and, who knows, it might help to bring them down.'

Ash did not imagine for a minute that his schoolboy stunt would pay off.

A few moments later, Carey Merino rushed in.

'Ash. We've got them. My guys have just told me that Peters and Copthorne were arguing yesterday with Mrs Peters about what to do with Doug. They're holding him at Mike Peters's house. I'm going to call the police and get them to raid the place.'

'What do we do about Peters and Copthorne in the meantime?' Ash asked.

'You do nothing. Let them carry on and I'll get the police over here.'

Carey Merino left and, as the delegates trooped back in for the final session, Peters and Copthorne strolled by, signalling to Ben they'd be back in two minutes.

'They're going to the loo, Ash. Do you seriously want me to turn their mics on?'

'Oh why not, let's do it,' said Ash.

*　　*　　*

Peters: *Gavin Boatwright's arrest gives us a major fucking problem.*

Copthorne: *What are we going to do now about Doug Bonsall?*

Peters: *You're going to have to dispose of him from your boat.*

Copthorne: *I'll make a damn sight better job of it than you did with William Cloudesley. Why the hell did you leave his body to rot in the water cistern? Bloody hopeless! Why did you kill him, anyway?*

Peters: *We had to silence him. You agreed. After we'd roughed him up a bit, he told us about all the files he'd given to that bloody woman and her boyfriend Bonsall. He even told us he'd given them incriminating information about Boatwright and that's why we tipped off that shit. How was I to know Boatwright would take matters into his own hands. He said he'd dispose of both the girl and Bonsall, but now he's been arrested we'll have to deal with Bonsall ourselves.*

Copthorne: Boatwright will talk. I think we're done for. We might as well let Bonsall go and take our chances. We're in the clear over the woman's death after all and you say there's nothing connecting us to Cloudesley's murder.

Peters: Fiona was seen talking to Bonsall. That's another problem we've got. She and I agreed in advance that if he came to the party she'd offer to give him some files on the Bond and CaBRe, but only if he went home with her. It worked. He agreed and she gave him some old accounts to look at. He tried to leave with them, so she hit him over the head with a bottle of Black Rum. He was just coming round when I arrived back home. He'll say she lured him to our place by offering him information about the Bond, but we can say he and Fiona were having an affair. There was an accident and I overreacted and tied him up until I could figure out what to do with him.

Copthorne: It'll all come out, Peters. You're an absolute ruddy fool. I'm ruined.

Peters: *Well, we still have to go back in and face those deadbeat delegates. Let's worry about what to do next when this blasted conference is over and done with.*

*   *   *

'After you, Wallace,' said Peters as they walked back into the conference room. 'Let's get this show back on the road.'

They were both startled to hear those same words echo loudly throughout the pin-drop silent room.

After just a few steps, they looked at each other for a moment, realising what must have happened, and bolted for the door.

Ash, Ben, Carey Merino and the two technical assistants had already moved to block their exit.

*   *   *

Mike Peters and Wallace Copthorne were escorted outside to await the arrival of the police.

Ash went onto the podium and apologised to the delegates for the disruption caused.

This has been an interesting week. I want to thank you all for coming to Bermuda. I can't say any more about what you heard being discussed between Mike Peters and Wallace Copthorne, although I'm sure you'll draw your own conclusions. Watch this space for further developments. This year's Bermuda Biennial has officially closed. A light buffet lunch is being provided for anyone interested.

As soon as Ash finished speaking, there was a hubbub as delegates rushed to talk to their immediate neighbours about the dramatic revelations they'd overheard.

19.

SATURDAY

By the time Ash, Dawn and Ben were ready to head to the airport for the late evening flight to Gatwick, a lot had happened:

Mike Peters and Wallace Copthorne were under arrest for the murder of William Cloudesley, the kidnapping of Doug Bonsall and their fraudulent activities in connection with the Bermuda Bond and CaBRe.

Harriet Hall was being held on the charge of running a brothel and blackmail.

Gavin Boatwright was charged with the murder of Beatrice Goode.

Carey Merino – having briefly examined the papers found on Gavin Boatwright's yacht – said he was going to open an investigation into drug running, racketeering, money laundering and fraud. He thanked Ash for all his help and apologised that two deaths had not been averted.

Following Doug Bonsall's rescue, it was agreed that he would help both the Bermuda Police and the FBI to develop their cases.

Eddie Wilkins undertook to work with Doug to plan the release of the Bermuda Papers, anonymously, for international press scrutiny. He decided to stay on the island to help not only with this but also with matters related to Bee's death.

Dorian Miller was cleared and released from custody. The Dockyard immediately offered him his job back, but he said he'd decided to take some leave to consider his future and whether or not he wished to remain on Bermuda.

Selwyn Brookes thanked Ash for the conference and told him he was actually relieved to be getting rid of Wallace Copthorne and Mike Peters as he'd never liked either of them. Contemplating likely insolvency fee income, he said he greatly looked forward to both the liquidation of CaBRe, and the Bermuda Bond being wound up.

*   *   *

On the plane back to London, Ash wondered if his own bond with Bermuda was broken and whether he would only be returning to the island if asked to do so by the authorities.

Also from Thorogood

www.thorogoodpublishing.co.uk

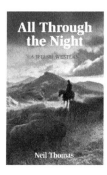

All Through the Night

ISBN paperback: 978 185418 8960
ISBN eBook: 978 185418 8977

Written in the style of an old-fashioned Western, this tale of Welsh drovers taking a large herd of cattle from North Wales to London in the 1790s, stakes a claim for these engaging characters to be considered the first 'cowboys'.

Running through this 'Welsh Western', which is rich in adventures and incidents, the storyline has the strong cultural, emotional and human elements that make Westerns so appealing in exploring how people act in the drama of their own lives.

Keeping the Lid On

ISBN paperback: 978 185418 8984
ISBN eBook: 978 185418 8991

Set in a private school a little in the past – at a time of turbulence following the death of the Old Headmaster – a sinister thread runs through the attempts to take the School forward. In whose best interests are the figures in authority acting; their own or those in their care?

Spy Without a Cause

ISBN paperback: 978 185418 9127
ISBN eBook: 978 185418 9134

With a background of corruption and tax avoidance, this intricate novel is set against events in the early 1980s in Britain's Hong Kong, the Manila of Marcos and Lee Kuan Yew's Singapore.

A young publisher is confronted with personal greed, kleptocracy, espionage and murder as matters move, Eric Ambler style, out of his control.

The Missing Monsieur Max

ISBN paperback: 978 185418 9141
ISBN eBook: 978 185418 9158

The disappearance of an Englishman in Southern France is investigated by Avignon's answer to Maigret, Commandant Ruppert, who delves into the lives of those connected with the missing man.

Set in 2006 in St Rémy de Provence, with the location itself as much a character as those he interviews, Ruppert is given the case to solve after a false start by the local police.

Playing Popular Piano and Keyboards

ISBN paperback: 978 185418 9165

Are you afraid of the piano or keyboards? Do they conjure up visions of endless lessons, finger-stumbling exercises, incomprehensible staves of unplayable scales and that depressing feeling that you would never be able to play what you like best?

Set out in straightforward lesson form, this book gives an easy-to-follow method of understanding chords and of using them to play from sheet music, by ear and for improvising.

The book is written and structured to make it suitable for beginners, 'classical pianists' and all those who once had lessons – and gave up. It can also be used as a teaching aid.

Available at Amazon and all good retailers.